In Love and Free

The tale of a woman caught between two men...

notionpress.com

In Love and Free

The tale of a woman caught between two men...

Jagdish Joghee

notionpress.com

Notion Press

Old No. 38, New No. 6

McNichols Road, Chetpet

Chennai - 600 031

First Published by Notion Press 2015

ISBN: 978-93-5206-319-2

*For enduring all the hardship and incessantly working behind the scene. To the one who inspires me - **Moni***

Also from the Author,

The Colour of Love

A Stranger by the Stream

The Bovine Redemption

Foreword

The sea is intriguing and exciting. It always reinforces in me a sense of belonging. The waves bring with them a strange kind of peace and calm. The sea has been a silent spectator to many major incidents in my life – the many outings with friends and family; the long walks on the shore with dad, my hero and philosopher; the moments spent with my love – the memories are endless. Through melancholy and bliss, this magnificent body of water has given me the kind of courage that no human being has ever given. It has embraced me during the most challenging moments of my life. All my worries dissolve in the foamy waters of the unending ocean. The waves bring with them immense strength and bliss; each time their foam touches my feet, these virtues are imbibed in me. My love for the mighty ocean will remain strong forever.

As I sit and watch the sea for the millionth time in my life, I reminisce about my life and realise how kind my stars have been. It was along another shoreline of the same Indian Ocean that my life underwent a major upheaval. And what a blow that was!

Chapter - 1

What is the first thing that strikes you when you think of love? What comes to my mind is the image of this tall and handsome man with wheatish skin. He was my first love. I met him when I was twenty years old and he had swept me off my feet like no other man had before. I had never been so crazy about anybody my entire life. In fact, I had not even met any good-looking man till then. However, this man had more than just good looks. His soft-spoken nature, his gentle approach and maturity that surpassed his age, reminded me of my dad. He was also a good dancer. I had always found men who could dance or write very attractive. After twenty years on earth, I had finally met a man who was perfect. The initial attraction slowly turned into mad love and then total devotion. He soon became an inseparable part of my life. But how do I let go of him?

Madhan Ponnappa Pemmaiah belonged to the powerful Kodava community in Coorg. His family was in the realty business in Bangalore. Madhan was 5 feet 10 inches tall and had looks to die for. But not all girls in college agreed with me. In our class of thirteen girls, only two of us found him attractive. He was not the kind of person who worked out at the gym. His most striking feature was his intelligence. He even challenged the professors on some of the most complex theories. We both competed with each other in class. Our friendship that started with sharing notes, studying together, and doing projects together gradually grew stronger and turned into love.

We met in Pune while doing our master's in business administration at the Symbiosis Institute of Management. Both our families wanted us to gain some business knowledge before we took over our respective family businesses. Our parents reasoned that we didn't have to go out and work when we had a business empire waiting to be taken over.

I belonged to an affluent Nair family from Kerala, which had settled down in Chennai. I had no siblings but that never mattered to me. I was always impeccably groomed. I often went to an upscale salon to pamper myself. I loved my hair and enjoyed getting it styled every four weeks. Facials and hair treatments were also mandatory. My family and friends loved my dimpled smile. Madhan thought I resembled the Bollywood actress Kangana Ranaut. I took that as a compliment. She was one of my favourite actresses. I thought she was one of the few intelligent actors in the country. Madhan often said that I was both intelligent and beautiful like Kangana. I loved the way he looked at me whenever I was dressed well. But it was not just my good looks that attracted him. Well, that is what he said to me and I believed him.

I still remember the day Madhan declared his love for me. We sneaked out of college after the first hour and headed straight to Lonavla on the Mumbai-Pune Expressway. We had heard about how romantic this place was and what a perfect getaway it was for a date. Madhan drove the car while I sat next him holding his arm throughout the drive. I will never forget this moment. There was so much romance, calmness and love between us.

Though it was a weekday, we saw many couples. Romance was in the air. The weather was a big bonus. There was a slight hint of fog. The clouds that had gathered in the sky protected us from the sun. A chill breeze kept blowing, making our date unforgettably romantic. We spoke for a while, smiled at each other a lot and walked around with our arms around each other. We settled down behind a big rock so that people could not see us. Not that we were worried about them, but we wanted to be careful and not send out any wrong message to the others. For even a loving romantic embrace can appear vulgar in the eyes of many.

I settled in Madhan's arms. I was holding him tight. Our eyes met and a never-before feeling entered our hearts. We gazed at each other longingly. We were indeed smitten by each other. Even before we realised, our lips locked. Ah, my first kiss. I had heard stories of how the first kiss is etched in one's memory forever. This was absolute bliss. I felt a sense of belonging, a sense of togetherness. We kissed for a while and then Madhan took me by surprise with his proposal of love for me. Those magical words still linger in my heart. We knew that we both loved each other, but the proposal gave us a special feeling. My dream of finding the right man had become a reality.

The memorable day was marred by a loud thud. There was a head-on collision between a Maruti 800 and a Tata Indica. The whole place became quiet. Both the cars tumbled. We saw a couple in each car; they were screaming for help. I was shocked and started to shiver as people pulled out the couples who lay in a pool of blood. One of them was not moving and people in the crowd started murmuring about a 'certain' death.

Madhan held me close as he realised that I was not able to tolerate the gory accident. He kept his calm and took me away immediately. He started his car and we left the place. We hardly spoke through the ride. We stopped only after we reached a coffee shop in the city. By then, I had regained my composure. I started to talk. Noticing that I was fine, Madhan broke down. I realised that he had kept his calm only because he did not want to make me more nervous than I already was. He had tried so hard to be brave and strong. That day was important to me for two reasons. The first reason was the kiss and the proposal. Secondly, I realised that Madhan would never let me down during a crisis. He was a godsend. I had finally found a match to my dad.

Chapter - 2

After MBA, we soon found jobs in Pune through campus placements. We were not too keen on going abroad. Since we were among the best students, we had a say in where we wanted to work. Recruiters were only happy to give us a job in Pune although some tried to persuade us to take up jobs overseas. But we both joined McKinsey & Company in Pune as business analysts.

Both our families lined up several rich and smart suitors in a bid to get us married but we did not relent. Our love was strong and pure. We could even die for each other. We decided that if our families did not accept our love, we would walk away from all the wealth that we would have otherwise inherited. It was a tough fight but we were strong and our love was stronger. Finally, our parents gave in and we got married in Guruvayoor, Kerala.

For the wedding, I was dressed in a traditional white Kerala sari. Madhan wore a white shirt and a dhoti. The wedding was followed by two big receptions in Chennai and Bangalore. It seemed as though both families were competing with each other to establish who was the wealthier of the two.

I wore a red and golden beige designer sari for the first reception and a black sari interspersed with shades of sea green for the other reception. The heavily embellished saris were designed by the renowned Indian designer Sabya Sachi. Madhan opted for a Kiton K-50 suit specially designed in Italy for the Bangalore reception. For the other reception, he wore a light green and white *kurta* custom-made by a group of design students from the National Institute of Fashion Technology in Chennai. Since my dad was in the diamond business, I wore some of the costliest and prettiest diamond jewellery. The who's who of the political and business world attended both the events. I had dreamt of my wedding day all through the two years of MBA and four years of working in Pune. It was a surreal affair. It felt as if I was living a fairy tale.

The very next day after the reception in Bangalore, we set off to Europe. We had fifteen awesome days of romance, passion and wild sex. Those were the best days of my life. It was absolute bliss. We had sex every day and it was never boring. It felt new even though our first sexual experience had happened six years ago during the final year of college. But even after six years, it felt fresh. Our honeymoon was a reinvigoration of sorts of our sex life. Our days started with sex and ended with sex.

When we got tired of making love in our room at the Marriott Marbella Beach Resort in Spain, we decided to have some fun and adventure outdoors. We went out to the beach at 10 p.m. Though there were many people lounging on the shore, there were also several trees that offered privacy.

We quickly slipped out of our clothes behind a tree and had crazy wild sex for the next hour or so. Forbidden sex is always thrilling. It was so cold but we didn't give a damn. I wanted to scream in joy but I had to control myself. I ended up biting my fingers instead. I screamed and moaned so much that Madhan had to yell at me to shut up.

We poured our favourite Castello di Ama wine all over our bodies. We tried out all kinds of things that were kinkier than scenes from a porn movie. High on vodka and cocktails, we tried every possible position. We wanted to celebrate our union, after overcoming our family's stiff opposition. We wanted to celebrate in style, in the dirtiest, craziest way possible.

We were exhausted after our adventurous sexual sojourn. We lay on the sand till midnight recollecting our wonderful days at college and work. My life couldn't get any better, I thought.

The rest of the honeymoon was spent visiting Mundaka and Zarautz in Spain and Biarritz and Hossegor in France. We then headed to Italy for more breathtaking romance, pizzas, and boat rides. We went surfing, trekking, paragliding and snorkelling. Being great foodies, we tried out every possible local dish – *espeto de sardinas* in Spain, *duck confit* and *croque-monsieur* in France, *osso buco* and Tuscany pizzas in Italy.

At Florence, Italy, we were fortunate to witness a fabulous display of fireworks during the Calcio Storico Fiorentino celebration. We also watched rugby, soccer and wrestling as part of the celebrations.

Of all the places we visited, Tuscany in Italy stood out. Be it the rolling hills, mountain paths, or the seaside, this place had something for every tourist. We had some fabulous wine here; Tuscany's food too was second to none. The people were warm and accommodating.

As our honeymoon came to an end, I told Madhan that we had to visit these places again during our old age.

Chapter - 3

When we returned to India, we decided to continue working since our family businesses were in different parts of the country. Madhan was a gentleman and never once suggested settling down in Bangalore. He also never said he would not move to Chennai if I decided to take up my dad's business. I liked him for not imposing his views on me. I saw many of my friends going through a rough time in their marriage. I had never seen him flirt with any girl in college or office. I was even ready to forgive him if he flirted with a woman. He was too perfect and I could only compare him to the Supreme Being. There are certain things in life that money cannot buy and Madhan was one of them. I was very lucky to have him in my life.

I soon got pregnant with twins. Our little prince charming and princess darling came into the world on 21 October, 2010. It was one of the most joyous moments of our life. Our family doctor once remarked that one must witness child birth to experience the presence of God. When I was giving birth, through all the pain, I felt… Well, I cannot even find the right word to explain my feelings. We had never seen our parents this happy before. We were one happy family and I knew we would live happily ever after. What more could a girl ask for?

An affluent family, top class education, romance with the most eligible gentleman on earth, a job at a top consulting company, a beautiful marriage, and a boy and girl at the same time… I had it all. I thanked the Almighty endlessly.

Due to his dad's sudden poor health, Madhan had to take over his family business. I had quit my job during the last trimester of my pregnancy. I moved to Chennai and stayed with my parents till my children were six months old. All through these years, I always knew I would end up in Bangalore. Given Madhan's passion for business, this was a given. Since my dad was in good health, there was no pressing need for me to take over his business. That was still a good decade or so away.

I moved to Bangalore to live with my in-laws. The joint family set-up meant Madhan and I didn't have much time together alone. We had been just the two of us for a long time. I had enjoyed so much freedom, moving around the house in shorts and sometimes just a bikini. Initially, it was difficult for me to adjust to the new life. I had to be dressed in a salwar kameez or sari most of the time. It bugged me a lot.

Of course, Madhan wanted me to be myself and not give up my identity just for the sake of his parents. But I did not think it would be appropriate to continue dressing the way I had before. Madhan's parents were great people. They treated me like their own daughter. Madhan's mother once told me that she had always wanted to have a daughter but that had never materialised.

Soon my life got better. All my apprehensions about living with in-laws went up in smoke. I had heard several stories from my friends about fights with in-laws that even led to divorce.

But I had no reason to worry. I also vowed that no matter what happened, I would adjust.

With twins to take care of, I had long sleepless nights. Thankfully, we had three domestic helps to take care of the house. At night, my mother-in-law slept in our room to help me. After feeding both the babies at the same time, I was drained of all energy. Breastfeeding twins was very demanding. My days started and ended with exhaustion. Motherhood was exciting, enthralling and frustrating at the same time.

Despite help from all quarters, I hardly had time to breathe. I wanted to be a hands-on mom and did not hire a nanny to take care of my children. I thought this was a woman's biggest responsibility and pleasure too. I did not want to share it with anyone. During these anxious days, my mother-in-law was of great help. Madhan slept in another room. Since he worked late, he had to get enough sleep. While I did miss him, I did not want to ruin his sleep. The best part of the day was doing yoga with Madhan in our lush balcony overseeing the beautiful Ulsoor Lake. I would wait for this one hour all day long. This was the only time we had together, alone. Our sex life took a backseat. We made love once or twice a month. It was not a big deal for both of us. We reconciled to the new reality of life.

Madhan made it a point to take me out at least once a month. We usually unwound at the Zulu pub on M. G. Road. We would dance to glory after a couple of drinks. Sometimes we went to the movies or dinner. On some weekends, we would go out as a family with Madhan's parents and our kids. Life had indeed changed but for the better. I was enjoying every bit of my role as a wife, a mother, and a daughter-in-law. I had a life that thousands of women only dreamt about. I had it all on a platter.

The first two years of motherhood were tough but also enjoyable. I was too busy raising the kids. This gave Madhan time to focus on his business and his ambition of becoming the number one realtor in the state of Karnataka.

Chapter - 4

I loved the apartment we were staying in. It was a beautiful apartment located just a few metres away from the Ulsoor Lake. The apartment complex had four blocks. Three blocks were named A, B and C. The three-storied fourth block was a recreational complex facing the lake. It housed a tennis court. There was a gymnasium on the first floor. The second floor had a library and table tennis and badminton courts. The third floor was empty and could be used by the people in the apartment complex for classes or events for a fee.

One part of the third floor opened into a balcony from where one could see the beautiful Ulsoor Lake and a tank that hadn't been used for many years (a bigger and better tank had been constructed on the rear side of the apartment). The balcony was used more like a hideout. Madhan and his friends from the apartment used this space for drinks sometimes. We heard voices from the balcony but no one could be seen. Madhan described the place as a "shady hideout for unmonitored activities." In the middle of the blocks was a beautiful garden laden with neem trees; there was also a swimming pool that was four metres deep and a children's play area with slides, swings, ladders and see-saws.

Encompassing the swimming pool was a large club house to host functions, parties and other fun activities. We could use the club house for a small fee. The apartment complex also had a Ganesh temple, a departmental store, a unisex salon, and a car wash garage. This was not just another community. It was like living in a luxurious resort. I preferred this kind of a residential complex with all amenities. I had insisted on Madhan buying this apartment though he wanted an independent house. But I always had my way with him. While this apartment was more expensive than an independent house, the amenities were worth the extra cost.

This was one of the most vibrant and happening apartments in the city. It was different from the other apartments. The members of the governing committee were always on their toes, planning several activities through the year. We looked forward to Diwali, New Year, Holi and Christmas celebrations. They were a lot of fun and we danced till we dropped. Also, there was always delicious food to binge on. In the evenings, it was not just the play area that would teem with mothers and children. Right next to the play area was a badminton court. It was always crowded. The indoor badminton court was for the pros and the outdoor one was used by all and sundry for fun. Four people, across all age groups, formed a team and played against four other people. We called this 'funminton'. We would queue up to get a shot at the game. The apartment complex also had a volleyball court on the far side of the garden. Eight to ten members would team up to play the game. It was always fun and frolic at this apartment complex.

The men in the complex were mostly decent, barring the odd one or two men who stared at women's breasts or their bodies. Lecherous men existed everywhere in the world. Money and education did not make any difference.

In this respect, Madhan was a respectful man. So was Rahul, our neighbour and family friend. He always spoke to women looking into their eyes. Though I had a good rapport with most people in the apartment thanks to my outgoing nature, Rahul and Meera were the closest of them all. They made a great couple. They had an adorable three-year-old daughter, Tina. They lived in the block next to ours on the third floor. They had moved in when Tina was a year old. Rahul worked at a top IT firm in the city. He was part of the management at the firm. Meera was a doctor and worked for a hospital close to our apartment. We began bonding with each other over conversations at the play area where our children played in the evenings.

Tina was like my third child. With both parents working, she came over to my place a lot. Rahul and Meera had a help who took care of Tina but I would often go to their house to check on Tina, and I would often bring her home.

Tina started playschool along with my children Ashita and Ashwin. Rahul and I took turns to pick them up from school. Sometimes, we would go together. Rahul's office allowed flexible work hours. Another reason why Rahul was keen on joining me was because he loved my car, a Mercedes Benz Sport E Class 350. Rahul had a fascination for cars and he enjoyed driving my Benz a lot.

Rahul, Meera, Madhan and I hung out with each other a lot. We went out together and also had lunch and dinner at each other's place. We were one big family. My blessings just kept increasing every day. I often told Madhan that in my previous birth, I must have been an exceptionally kind soul with several good deeds to my credit to be blessed with such a wonderful life in this birth.

Chapter - 5

When Ashita and Ashwin started going to playschool at three years, my in-laws insisted that I should get involved in Madhan's business at least for a few hours a day.

They didn't want me to stay at home all the time. But I was not interested in Madhan's business.

I was extremely interested in Zumba though. It had been my favourite pastime before pregnancy. I loved the mad rush of endorphins in my body after each work-out. After I got pregnant, I took up yoga. I had always been a good dancer but I had never pursued it seriously. During my MBA days, I had been a star dancer at all cultural events. Cheers from the crowd still reverberated in my ears.

Zumba is one of the best exercises to help you get into shape quickly. So, I underwent a three-month training at the Zumba Institute on Banerghatta Road. After completing the training, I decided to start teaching Zumba. I discussed this with the women in the apartment. They were eager to learn Zumba. So, thirteen women signed up for a two-hour class that started at 10 a.m. This was the most convenient time for most home-makers.

The training involved warm-up and cool-down sessions. There were three sessions a week. The fee was Rs 1000 a month. Money was not my primary interest. I took this money to issue pamphlets, buy CDs, and provide refreshments. Though the women found it hard in the beginning, they got used to the moves gradually.

Unlike working out in the gym, cycling or swimming, Zumba can never get mundane. We don't do the same thing again and again. We invent new steps and make it fun and enjoyable. While there is Zumba-specific music, I preferred hit numbers in Hindi, Kannada, Tamil and English. I mixed up the music and choreographed the moves accordingly. This was an instant hit with all the women. My class strength grew slowly and steadily through word-of-mouth. I became an overnight star in the apartment complex, especially among the men as they were happy to see their wives get back in shape. While I primarily trained women, I also had a few men in the class. Sandeep, Rahul and Chetan.

Rahul had insisted on learning Zumba. He even dragged his friends along with him. He was a good friend and I could not say no to him. Since I had no extra time to spare, the men joined the women. They were disciplined students. All three men were from the IT industry, which allowed them flexible working hours. They also had the option to work from home. This work culture amazed me. I wished all sectors allowed this. We would then have more happy people in the country.

Soon, Rahul and I became good friends. On the days that Rahul attended Zumba class (he tried to make it twice a week), we would drive together to the playschool to pick up Ashita, Ashwin and Tina. Some days, we would take the children to an ice-cream parlour or coffee shop. Going to school with Rahul helped because it was sometimes difficult to handle the three little cute devils alone.

Rahul and I played 'funminton'. We were not great at the game but we played decent enough to win a few games. There were times when we chased each other around the park with racquets in our hands. Sometimes, Rahul mistimed his shots and the shuttlecock would smack me from behind. Meera looked after our children while we had our share of fun. She chatted endlessly with her friends unmindful of what we were up to.

One day, Rahul and I created a record of sorts by dancing for an hour continuously, without any break. We usually took frequent breaks. Rahul was very happy and carried me with joy. It was no mean achievement. So, all of us from class went to the Costa coffee shop near our apartment and treated ourselves to some lovely brownies, French chocolate, and chillers.

Madhan tried his best to make up for the lost time with family. But with the housing market slowing down and investments taking a backseat, the going was indeed tough. It was a question of survival of the fittest and Madhan had to put in extra time and efforts to bring in profits. He was determined to get through this phase somchow. He believed that the country's prospects would improve in the years to come.

We had planned to go to Brazil on a holiday, coinciding with the football world cup. But with Madhan working hard, we had to cancel the trip.

We hadn't been on a holiday for more than three years. Our sex life had slowed down dramatically. In fact, the time we spent together had also reduced drastically. But I had no complaints. I wanted to support Madhan in every step.

Chapter - 6

I was dressed in a royal blue and green georgette sari, which I had bought in Mumbai while accompanying Madhan on one of his business trips a few months ago.

Madhan asked me to let my hair loose and wear a big blue bindi. I obliged. He knew exactly how to dress up for what occasion. I often teased him that he had picked up his sartorial sense from his girlfriends. Given his eye for fashion, many girls vied for his attention. Madhan too liked attention from others. This sometimes irritated me, but we had great trust in each other. My mom always used to tell me, "If your spouse wants to cheat on you, he or she will. This world is a haven of opportunities. But no matter what, in any relationship, one must never doubt the spouse."

Madhan could do anything during the ten to twelve hours he was out at work or during his business trips. But it was our love that held us together and I knew this would last a life time.

Diwali was a happening festival in my apartment. No one went to their hometown or any other place. For this Diwali, I persuaded my parents to come over to Bangalore. It was the perfect time for a family get-together. The children were excited. But they were also scared with all the noise around.

Rahul and Meera too had a full house with Meera's parents, her brother's family, and Rahul's sister's family. They all lived in Bangalore.

That evening, I had invited all of them to our apartment.

Everyone, including Madhan, was out in the open watching the fireworks. I was getting delayed as I had to do my hair according to Madhan's wish. I was happy to let my hair loose and look pretty for him. Madhan took great pride in flaunting me before his friends, colleagues and family. I liked the attention, but never once did he treat me like a trophy wife.

As I was looking for the house keys, Rahul walked in. He had come in for the box of crackers that had been left behind in the store room. I quickly took out the box and gave it to him. As we were leaving the house, Rahul looked at me and said, "Wow! I have never seen you look this beautiful before."

Rahul was one person who didn't hold himself back. He always spoke his heart.

I smiled at him and said, "So, was I not beautiful all these years, Mr Big Mouth?"

Rahul laughed and held my hand. This was not new. We danced together. We had also hugged each other a few times. So, Rahul holding my hand meant nothing. He then looked into my eyes and said, "You are one of the prettiest women I know. But today, you look out of the world."

As he said these words, I felt strange. It felt unusual. I could not take my eyes off him. He continued. "At this moment, my heart is thumping wildly and my mind is telling me to hold you close to me."

He came closer to me and whispered in my ears, "I don't know if this is right or wrong. But, at this moment, as I look at you I am struggling to hold back my feelings."

I couldn't speak a word. He lifted my chin and held my face. I held his arms, and even before I could realise anything, we kissed. The moment was intense. Our tongues twirled and twisted around each other. It was pure magic. There was love. As we let go of each other's mouth, I rested on his chest. We held each other tight. Nothing else mattered to us at that moment. No amount of noise from the crackers could disturb us. Those few minutes were reminiscent of my first kiss with Madhan. They reminded me of the wonderful days of love, passion, excitement and endless joy.

I looked up to Rahul and said, "What is this? I cannot believe this. I have not had such feelings towards you from the time I have known you. Aren't we cheating on our partners?"

Rahul lifted my chin again and looked me in my eyes. I couldn't speak a word. I closed my eyes. And we kissed again. We bit each other quite a few times. I held him close. My breasts were pressed against his chest. He put his hands around my hip, bringing me closer. I loved it. My body was simmering for more. I liked the tingle in my nerves and enjoyed the chill running down my spine. I wanted more of this. Rahul was a great kisser and I couldn't help but draw comparisons with Madhan's kissing. Madhan's kisses were soft. He treated me like a dainty flower in bed.

Then a pang of guilt hit me. "What am I doing?" I wondered. We were running out of time. We had to go down as both our families were waiting for us. But I didn't want to let go of this moment. It brought back memories of my college days when I would be lost in Madhan's embrace for hours together. I remembered the first day we made love in Madhan's flat. All those wonderful moments kept flashing in my head. I was transported to a whole new world. Then, Rahul brought me back to this world. He held my chin and as I looked up into his eyes, he whispered, "Shruthi, I love you." My world shattered hearing those words. "What the hell have I gotten myself into?" I shuddered.

I was quiet all evening. Rahul kept looking at me and I tried to avoid every bit of him. Both our families went out for dinner to the Citrus restaurant at the Lemon Tree hotel on St John's Road near Ulsoor Lake. During dinner, Rahul managed to find a seat next to me. He tried to strike a conversation with me, but I just wasn't myself.

That night was the longest night of my life. The guilt in me was driving me insane. I cried all night and managed to get very little sleep. I woke up late the next morning. Madhan was already off to work. I hoped Rahul had got the message from my silence during dinner. But that was not to be. Catastrophe struck again. I saw my mobile phone beep. A message from Rahul read, "Good morning, sweetheart."

"Oh God, why are you doing this to me?" I thought to myself.

I cursed myself. Playing with the children and helping my mother-in-law in the kitchen helped distract myself from stray thoughts about Rahul. When I spoke to Madhan on the phone, I felt relieved. This was a regular practice. Every time my thoughts drove me crazy, I called Madhan just to hear his reassuring voice. After the call with Madhan, I saw that there were ten messages from Rahul. They were all romantic ones. Did he not get the message? I was not responding to his text messages. Did he not get it yet? I decided to ignore his messages and talk to him in person instead.

That evening, I was out with the kids in the park. Rahul and Meera joined me. I smiled at them. Our eyes met again.

I felt so bad. I didn't have the courage to look at Meera. I wondered how Rahul didn't have even an iota of regret. I knew he was in the park only because I was around.

After some time, I got some time alone with Rahul when Meera went to the pool area to speak to someone. Rahul came close to me and tried to hold my hand. I pulled away. I gathered my guts and told him, "Rahul, I am sorry. I don't know what happened to me yesterday but this is not right. I look at Madhan, Meera, and our kids and I feel so guilty. I just want to forget all this and go back to being what we were. Please."

Rahul didn't say a word. He kept looking at me. "Rahul, please don't make me feel uncomfortable. Say something."

What he said left me speechless. "The very first time I saw you two years ago, I fell in love with you. You are the only one that my heart has skipped a beat for. I never mentioned this earlier because I thought this was insane and I would only be ruining our relationship. But yesterday when I saw you and the way you looked…" He paused for a moment and said, "You were dazzling. I just couldn't hold back."

"Fine! It was a spur of the moment thing, Rahul, and I am equally to blame. But why the proposal of love? We could have stopped with the kiss. Why did you send all those messages? At least now can you put an end to this? Think about your family. You will never find a partner as perfect as Meera."

"I do love Meera and my kid. They are my world and I will not lose them for anything. I am sorry, Shruthi. But…"

"So, you guys talking about that management shit again eh?" interrupted Meera.

"Nah, we were just trying to resolve a complex issue. More complex than any management theory," I said with a smile. The mess we had gotten ourselves into was probably the most complicated one in the world, I thought.

"Well, you and your complex management theories," said Meera, shrugging her shoulders.

After that, Rahul never found the right time to complete what he had started to say.

We went home after some time. There were no more messages from Rahul. I felt so relieved and thanked the Almighty for resolving the issue once and for all.

Madhan came home early that day. I had a quiet dinner with him. I asked him to take me out for a drive. We had an ice-cream at our favourite Cubbon Park parlour. I felt so warm and secure with him around. I wouldn't trade this feeling for anything else on earth. Once in bed, I held him close, looked at him, and said, "I love you, baby."

"I love you too, sweetie pie. Are you alright Mrs Shruthi Vasudevan Nair?" asked Madhan, giggling. Madhan was never in favour of me changing my surname and I was glad to retain my identity. We cuddled and kissed each other and made love. My world was a safe haven. There was no looking back. Yesterday was a bad dream and an isolated moment of madness in my otherwise blemish-free life. I was glad to let that go.

Chapter - 7

Six months later…

I was lying on top of the tank in my apartment terrace. It was a beautiful evening. It was 8 p.m. and the stars were out. There were no clouds around – just the sparkling stars that reminded me of my own self. The stars shone and sparkled in the night. They were lost during the day. I had become this two-faced person who pretended and lied to her family. Deceit had won over honesty and trust. I often lied to my husband with whom I once used to share even my weirdest thoughts. I started ignoring my children's needs. In the process, I let them become dependent on their grandparents. I fabricated stories to my family. I lied about where I was and when I would return home.

Rahul and I often met at the abandoned tank in my apartment block twice or thrice a week. We made out every time we met. We kissed and cuddled. We never went beyond this. We did not have the guts to completely surrender ourselves to each other. I was not yet ready to take our relationship to the next level. I was also not ready to take the risk of being spotted by someone. That would've been awkward and embarrassing. I liked making out with Rahul and I was happy with just that. Rahul insisted on sex a couple of times as he thought there was no chance of anyone seeing us, but I was not comfortable. I assured him that he would have me in full, but he had to wait.

One day, Rahul had to leave early as he had to pick Meera up from her clinic. We kissed for a while and Rahul said quietly, "Love you, baby." He then left. I smiled. It had taken me some time to come to terms with the relationship with Rahul. I was not in love yet. Rahul had to wait for that as well.

Rahul made it a point to proclaim his love at least ten times every time we met. Love is a wondrous feeling. I would know the moment it struck me again. I was already pretending a lot in life. I didn't want to fake love with Rahul.

The hypocrite hidden deep inside me slowly crept out. I could never tolerate it when girls in college or women in office got close to Madhan, even for professional reasons. Look at me now! I continued to play the part of a wife, but I was also somebody else's lover. My heart was torn between the two men in my life. I had become this rapacious person who wanted to have everything in life.

I needed time to take the relationship with Rahul to the next level simply because I couldn't risk losing Madhan. He was, is, and will always be the love of my life. I could understand Rahul's love for me because he had had an arranged marriage. So, he falling in love with me two years ago made sense, but I could not comprehend my love for him. Yes, I was not yet there in the real sense of the term, but I still could not fathom the reason for the lust and desire I had for him.

After the lapse on Diwali night, I tried my best to avoid Rahul. For two months, I managed to get on with life. But every time I met Rahul, I could not be myself. He looked lost too. He stopped attending the Zumba classes. He came to the play area occasionally to watch over his daughter or play badminton, but it was not like before. The fun and laughter had dried up. A couple of times Rahul said he planned to move to another area as he could not hold himself back seeing me every day. I did have a soft corner for him. Rahul admitted he had been leering at me for two years. Slowly, I started to fall for him and I could not hold myself back. I gave it a lot of thought and wondered if it was worth a shot. I knew it was not mere lust. I knew this was also about love and the heart's desire.

No matter how much I tried to justify the affair, the fact remained that I was a deceitful person. One moment I was making out with a man and an hour later I was in bed with another man. Who had I become? What had I lost in life that led me to do this? Did I not have a perfect life? Was I not happy? Of course, I was happy. I knew I was happy and content. Had I become greedy? I was in a maze and I could not find a way out.

But I found a way. It had a lot of thrill and needed some special skills to keep it going. Skills that enabled me to lie, create stories, and pretend to my family. God had always been kind to me all my life. I looked up the skies and asked him what he had in store for me. I had this perfect life. Was it his plan to ensure that human beings did not have a perfect life? I did not have the answers but I was willing to find them.

That evening, I entered my home rather late. I had completely lost track of time. The kids had fallen asleep with my in-laws. Madhan was watching TV. I sat next to him quietly. He didn't bother to ask me where I had gone and what

I had been doing. I had always enjoyed this freedom. But now I wished he had been possessive of me. I wish he hadn't trusted me this much. I wished he had hired a spy who watched every move of mine. We spent the next hour talking about his day. We then wrapped it up with dinner.

As I lay in bed trying to figure out the tangle I had gotten myself into, I realised temptation struck human beings in different forms. In the form of chocolates for children, drugs for young adults, bribe money for people in influential positions, and sometimes in the form of lust – like the kind I had been struck with. Human beings succumbed to this temptation despite knowing too well that they would suffer the consequences days, weeks, months or even years later.

My nights had become a nightmare. I didn't have happiness any longer. Was it true that people with the 'perfect' life often had a setback in order to have a 'complete' life? I thought of the celebrities who everyone thought had a 'perfect' life with success and happiness but let it all slip away. Was I in the same league as Tiger Woods, Lance Armstrong and Sanjay Dutt? I knew there was every chance I would get caught and suffer the consequences but I still wanted to go the full distance with Rahul. I wanted to see what God had in store for me.

Chapter - 8

Meera had to go to Sri Lanka for a doctors' conference from Monday to Friday. Rahul and Meera decided to make use of this opportunity and use the weekends for a vacation. Rahul wanted me to come too but I was not sure. I could not go without my husband and Madhan's business would not allow the luxury of taking off for so many days.

So, Rahul and I hatched a plan. Madhan could be with us on the weekends before and after the conference. From Monday to Friday, he could be in India to take care of his business. I knew Madhan would not have a problem with this as we had not been on a holiday since he took over the business from his dad. Madhan readily agreed to this plan. He would be with us for the first weekend and join us again for the next weekend after the conference.

This meant five week days of time alone for Rahul and I on a beach resort. We also made plans for the children. They would spend eight hours a day at the resort's programme for children. Rahul and I had to just peep in every now and then to check on them. This sounded thrilling. This would give me the opportunity to give myself fully to Rahul. I had made him wait for too long and it was not fair.

Madhan was so excited about the trip. The day we were leaving, he said to me, "I am so happy for you, sweetheart. I know I have not been able to take you out on a holiday but I am glad all this is happening on its own."

I smiled but my inner voice screamed, "It is not happening on its own. It's hatched. It's a conspiracy. I am betraying you, idiot. Can't you see that?"

"Madhan, that's fine. No holiday is complete without you," I said. And I meant it.

The first weekend in Sri Lanka was a complete family affair. Even my in-laws came. Surprisingly, Tina did not join us. She went to Meera's parents place in Hubli.

We stayed at the fabulous Taj Vivanta resort in Bentota, a small town about 40 km from Colombo. We drove from Colombo on one of the most scenic roads I had ever seen. The resort was splendid and the rooms were luxurious. We had booked three suite rooms. Rahul and I did not show even a hint of having an affair. We had agreed to dedicate the two days to our families. I loved the way Rahul agreed to all that I said. It gave me a feeling of being the boss. With the kids off with their grandparents, Madhan and I had a whale of a time in the evening. We sipped our favourite red wine, danced to our favourite tunes, ate yummy Sri Lankan fish curry, and finally hit the sack.

We went berserk in bed. It was crazy. We had the best sex of our life. This was much better than the wild sex we had had during our days in Pune. That night, we could not control ourselves. In the afternoon, we had fooled around inside the conference hall. I thought that was wild. But the night was even better. We kissed passionately, caressed each other calmly, and there was extended foreplay. That night, I had the best orgasm I've had in years. We rekindled our passion. We realised the importance of this emotional exchange. We spoke about our good old days, those magical years.

I asked Madhan if he thought I was spending less time with him and the kids. He said, "Be who you are and do what makes you happy." I was glad that he did not diminish my role as a wife and a mother. The affair with Rahul had made me guilty of not spending enough time with my family. But I realised that I spent only a few hours a week with Rahul. As Madhan went off to sleep, I walked out to the balcony and watched the sea rise and fall in harmony. I sat there quietly and wondered if this was the passion that had gone missing in our lives, leading me to Rahul. But if that was the case, then I would have slept with Rahul in the four months that we had been together. Why hadn't I been in bed with him? If passionate sex was what I needed, then I would have slept with Rahul months ago. We had our opportunities and we lived just blocks away from each other.

Meera had been out of station last month for a training programme in Mumbai. The kids were in the play area. Rahul and I had all the time. We made out but it never occurred to me to have sex. Rahul wanted it badly but I just wanted to spend time lying on his lap with his hands caressing my hair. I thought life was strange. Human needs were stranger. Sometimes, I wondered if we drew our own boundary line by being in a marriage, suppressing our feelings, emotions and needs. We think this boundary will keep us safe from others but seldom do we realise that it was an imaginary line that we had drawn for ourselves. It was something that human beings brought upon themselves. I for one had crossed the line.

I was one woman with Madhan and I was a completely different woman with Rahul. This was me. I didn't want to change that. I wanted it to last till the end of the world. Society and so-called values demanded that I kept the relationship with Rahul in the dark. So be it. I loved the dark and the secret fixation it brought with it. I quietly watched the waves forcing their way to the land; they retreated only to come back with force. I too like the waves wanted to keep trying to get ahead in life. I didn't want anything holding me back. I only hoped that as I moved ahead I would be able to hit the farther shores rather than recede. I was craving for love and an emotional embrace. I was drawing a dark path and I hoped this path remained in the dark. No one but Rahul and I would have access to the path all our lives.

Chapter - 9

We spent Sunday visiting the beautiful town of Galle. Standing on top of the majestic Galle Fort, we watched the sea in full splendour. We spent two hours at the fort, walking from one end to the other. Rahul was at his naughtiest best when he pinched my hip and planted a kiss on my cheek, when the others moved ahead. It was quick and brave. I glared at him and walked to my husband quickly. I was angry at Rahul's antics. But they were done and no one had noticed. So, I secretly enjoyed the moment. I recollected the days when Madhan and I were together during college and work. We never really cared for anyone. We did everything in the open. Everyone around us knew we were in a relationship. But this kind of hush-hush affair with Rahul, which could not be revealed at any cost, was exciting and intimidating at the same time. I felt like an adolescent girl, falling in love once again.

We visited the Galle cricket ground and took pictures. My husband said that Sri Lankan cricketer Muralidharan had claimed his record eight hundredth international wicket, playing his last test match, on this very ground. This was the reason an entire stand in the stadium was dedicated to him. Wow, I thought. I didn't care one bit; cricket was one game I loved to hate.

There was something about Sri Lanka that amazed me – its cleanliness. How clean Sri Lanka was, I thought. Every place I went to, from Colombo and Bentota to Galle, there was no litter in the public spaces. Sri Lanka may be a small country but there was still discipline. I wished we in India had this discipline and kept our towns clean and tidy.

On our way back to the hotel, we went to the turtle hatchery. The kids loved it. They tried to get their hands on every turtle possible. We spent a good hour here just for the sake of the kids. Then we headed to a beautiful seashore restaurant for lunch and had Sri Lankan fish curry. Sri Lankan dishes were just so yummy. I had never been treated to such fantastic fish curry all my life.

After spending the afternoon in our rooms, we headed to the Hikkaduwa beach in the evening. This beach was famous for surfing and boasted a beautiful coral sanctuary. Rahul bragged to us that he had arranged for a glass-boat ride and that we would be taken deep into the ocean to look at nearly 100 varieties of multi-coloured corals. We were all excited; the kids were over the moon.

We got on the glass-boat. But after a hundred metres, it stopped. Initially, we thought it was an engine failure but no. This was a sanctuary and we could go no further. The boat operator asked us to look through the glass; we saw numerous corals. As the operator kept the boat moving, we managed to see big fishes, turtles and other sea species. The kids were excited but we were disappointed. We thought we would go deep into the ocean. We had hoped to lose sight of the land and be surrounded only by water.

We all looked at Rahul. I knew he was going to be the butt of all jokes later, during dinner. Meera and my father-in-law took turns pulling his leg. Poor chap, he was not spared even by the kids. Madhan joined them too. I felt bad for him but kept mum.

This was one big happy family. I wished for this to last forever. I was surrounded by people who loved me, cared for me, and wanted only the best for me. Strangely, there was no feeling of guilt. Whoever said one man for one woman? Didn't the royals in the olden days marry as many times as they could to keep the clan expanding? Was it right for the royals and wrong for the commoners? Our scriptures elaborated the punishment for each crime. What was the punishment for lust? Whatever it was, it was a long time away. All I wanted was excitement and the path my hormones led me down.

Chapter - 10

Finally, the weekend was over. Madhan and his parents left for India early in the morning. I had had the best two days of my life with Madhan after a long time. I had enjoyed and lived every moment of it. Meera too left for her conference.

Rahul and I went with Ashita and Ashwin to the play zone. We spent an hour playing with the children. As the kids got comfortable with the environment and the other children (there were ten of them in total), we quietly slipped out. We told the kids that we would check on them now and then. We told them that Rahul had to do some office work and I had to practise Zumba. Of course, we both went straight to my room. Rahul wanted to go to his room, but I didn't want that. What if Meera came in earlier than expected? Rahul insisted on going to his room as he did have some office work.

"Bullshit," I said. I exerted my authority. "This is not the time to work, my boy. This whole trip was meant for us to be together; did you forget that?"

"Yes, I do remember. But I got a call from office this morning and they want me to get this presentation done by the afternoon. Please."

"You can bring your laptop over," I said. I stood my ground. I was clear. I would not take a chance. Rahul gave in and we ended up in my room.

Rahul was not happy though. I wondered why. He could work in my room. And I did have a point. It would be awkward if Meera dropped in.

Nevertheless, we had a good time.

I was wearing a sky blue, printed, shift dress with a racer back. Rahul was in a sleeveless T-shirt and beach shorts. This day was going to be special. I had decided to give him my all. Rahul held me by my arms and kissed me gently all over. He then lifted me gently and led me to the bedroom. I lay there with the sound of waves crashing the shore in the background. I was going to be crushed today. My hormones were going to rise and fall like the waves. Rahul was my shore and I would continue to seek him for the next few hours. The moment slowly took control over me. He undressed me slowly. As our lips locked, his hands slowly beseeched by breasts. I took his T-shirt off. His masculine body came in contact with my bare body.

God, did this moment wipe away all the guilt and pain of being in an extra-marital affair! I had an orgasm during foreplay. Rahul was more than good in bed. Lucky Meera, I thought. I understood the difference between having sex and making love. Sex was all about quenching one's hunger and thirst. It was about succumbing to one's hormones. Making love was about feeding the soul and the mind. It was about satisfying oneself both emotionally and physically. It was a celebration of love.

We swelled though the next half hour. I wanted more of this. Rahul let me be on top for the most part. I moaned and cried. As we lay down drenched in sweat, despite the air-conditioning, I realised this affair was not about sex. There was love. There was passion. It gave me pure joy and ecstasy. An ecstasy that was indefinable. Yes, I was in love. I was in love with two men. People may call me a whore but yes I was in love with two men. Today, a void had been filled. A void that was inexplicable. I kissed Rahul and whispered in his ears, "I love you." He was ecstatic.

"So I had to pass this physical examination to win you over, my love?"

"Ah, don't be a jerk. I had it in me, but I just felt like telling you now."

"Love you too, baby."

Rahul and I showered together. It was Rahul's idea. I was reluctant at first, but I went ahead with it anyway. He carried me to the shower. We lay in the bath tub, holding each other closely.

"I will never forget this day in my life, Rahul. You made me feel so special. You made me want more. This passion and joy will last for a lifetime."

We kissed again, showered together, and ended up making love one more time. It was amazing. I had lost myself once again in the love for a man.

I went to the kid's play area while Rahul headed to his room to complete his presentation. The kids were lost in their own world. They were enjoying the games, the magic show, and the toys. I sat there quietly and watched them play.

My mind recalled every second of what had happened earlier. I relished every bit. I knew I would savour the moment for a long time. Just then my son interrupted. "Mom, you bathed again? Did you get dirty?" He then went back to play with his new friends. These words struck me hard. "Did I get dirty?! Wow, was that true? Have I become dirty? Has my inner-being been dirtied forever?"

"No," I reminded myself. "You are reborn. You are not one of those who just want to live a content life. You are not among those millions who live in denial. You have the audacity to accept your love for two men. You scream from within that life is not all about being with one person. You are passionate about your feelings. You are emotional about your needs. You are not dirty. You have refreshed yourself. You are living a dream. Go on girl, conquer yourself."

I could not sleep all night. My mind was replaying the day. This was the first time my naked body had been revealed to a man other than Madhan. A year ago, I could not have imagined this. Madhan was the only one I had. I had strongly believed in the 'one-man-one-woman' concept. Today, I gave myself entirely to another man. Rahul had made my life come a full circle. I had a sense of fulfillment. This was not me. I had never wanted to have two men in my life.

The afternoons were not very adventurous as the kids needed to catch up on sleep. I also wound up next to them. By evening, Meera would return. We were all together till dinner and then retired to bed. Rahul and I had vowed not to give room even to the slightest suspicion. We made sure we behaved in the most appropriate manner in front of the children and Meera. That did not stop us from ogling at each other, winking, or sometimes even passing flying kisses to each other when no one was looking. This was like teenage, puppy love. Though mine was a love marriage, I hadn't experienced this kind of thrill. It was absolute fun. Rahul would kiss his glasses looking at me and I would get the chills. I would return his gesture by kissing one of my children and his face would glow with passion. It was crazy and thrilling.

Chapter - 11

The next three days were no different. We would make sure the kids settled down and then headed to my room. The time I spent with Rahul was no less than terrific. Rahul was so gentle, caring, and allowed me to be the boss. He had no qualms in letting me dictate my terms in bed. Every woman loved to be the dictator in bed as she alone knew what pleasured her the most. A man would never know; women could fake her orgasm to perfection. The joy of spending intimate moments with Rahul was infinite. I had multiple orgasms with him. We would talk for a long time after we were done, we would bathe together like kids. We would lock ourselves tight in one towel. I would lie on his chest like nothing else mattered in this world.

I felt like a woman who had broken all her shackles. I had no trouble keeping the relationship a secret in the dark. I loved every moment with my secret lover. I invariably started drawing comparisons with Madhan. I felt agitated whenever my mind engaged in these comparisons, but this was inevitable. The million-dollar question to which I had no answer even after pondering over it several thousand times was, what was lacking in Madhan that I found in Rahul? Nothing! Absolutely nothing!

The reason I wanted to keep my relationship with Rahul under wraps was for the fear of losing Madhan. That was not an option. I wanted both men in my life. The only conclusion

I could draw from this whole situation was that the 'one-man-one-woman' concept was a farce promoted by human beings who could not handle multiple relationships.

Either they did not have the ability or they believed multiple relationships were fake.

Rahul continued to show his displeasure about me refusing to meet him in his room. We had a few small arguments over this but it didn't take him too long to compromise. We didn't want to spoil our mood with petty fights. Rahul didn't hold on to his grudge for long, given that we had only these few days to be intimate. I was not sure about having sex with him once we got back to India.

But one day, the argument turned into a big fight. Rahul irritated me by not making any eye contact during dinner for two days. On Thursday evening, he did not come for dinner. Meera told me that he was held up with office work. I was angry. While Meera and the kids were having dinner, I excused myself and slipped out to the reception area to call Rahul's room. I asked him if he really had office work or he was angry with me. The whole thing sounded stupid to me.

"Rahul, we are not silly teenagers to fight over such issues," I told him.

"This may be a non-issue to you, Shruthi, but to me it's important. You say all this is so thrilling and you are living every moment of this. It's the same with me, Shruthi. I want to have my share of thrill. What's wrong with making love in my room?"

"I can't take chances, Rahul. Please understand." "We could get caught even in your room, babe."

"No point talking to you. Are you joining us for dinner? "I will if you agree to be in my room tomorrow."

"I will not."

"Then I cannot come for dinner." "Go to hell, Rahul."

I slammed the phone and returned to the restaurant.

Meera and I spent the next hour or so talking about a lot of things. She was a very good friend. I did have a pang of guilt but I was at a point of no return. There was no use feeling guilty about getting on to the ship when you were in the middle of the ocean. If you felt guilty or sorry, you had only one option — drown in the middle of the sea. But I loved this cruise with Rahul and I did not want to drown.

I hadn't seen Rahul all evening. I went to bed disappointed. We had had arguments and fights before but this was the first time we were going to bed without compromising or talking about it. I felt bad. Initially, I wondered why Rahul was making much ado about nothing. Then I started to blame myself. I had had it too easy in this relationship. I always had everything my way. Be it in India or here in Sri Lanka, Rahul had done everything the way I wanted. This was the only thing he asked for and I was being a jerk about it. I decided that I would go to his room the next day. Of course, there was the big risk of being caught by Meera. The last four days, she had come to the room only after 5 p.m. This was good enough data to depend on. I went to sleep thinking about the thrilling sex I would have the next day. It felt bizarre and frightening at the same time. One thing that worried me the most was, whenever I feared something, the worst possible event would occur. I hoped that this time I would be proven wrong.

Chapter - 12

The next day, Rahul was at breakfast. I was happy to see him. He did not smile at me or wish me. I kept quiet till Meera left. Once the kids were in the play area, I went next to Rahul and whispered, "Your room in thirty minutes flat." He just couldn't contain his joy. He guffawed and nearly lifted me. He was quick to come back to his senses. The kids asked him what he was up to. "It is a joke, kids. Now, continue playing."

We sat for some time in the play area and talked. It was nice to see Rahul in a good mood.

Just as we started to make our move towards his room, I heard a scream. "*Mamma.*" I turned back to see Ashita crying in pain. Rahul and I ran to her rescue. Ashita had hurt her leg badly while playing. Immediate medical attention was given and the hotel arranged for a doctor in fifteen minutes. After being given first-aid, she was advised to take rest. Rahul and I accompanied her to my room along with Ashwin. I put her to sleep and asked Rahul to take care of my son. As she slept, Ashita murmured, "*Mamma*, don't leave me please. Stay with me."

"I am not leaving you, sweetie," I consoled her.

Ashita had hurt herself badly and she was still not out of shock. After an hour, Rahul checked on us. Both my children had fallen asleep. Rahul wanted to know if we could sneak out for a bit and return. It hit me hard.

"Rahul, do you know that my daughter is in pain? When she wakes up, she will need me."

"I understand, Shruthi. I was just checking." "No dear. I am in no mood now."

We sat on the sofa. I rested my head on his shoulder. The children woke up in some time. Rahul quickly left for his room. I spent some time with the children and then took them out for lunch. Ashita was feeling much better. She could walk on her own. She just had to be careful not to hurt herself again. Rahul joined us for lunch. Both the children went to the nearby hall where a special magic show was being conducted. Being a Friday, the hotel was teeming with guests.

Rahul immediately pounced on this opportunity. We ensured the kids were well settled. The show would go on for three hours. We requested a hotel attendant to call me the moment my daughter asked for me. I knew this was our last opportunity in Sri Lanka. Once we were back in India, I did not know if we could ever be together. I hesitated a bit as I went with Rahul towards his room. As we walked past the reception area, we heard a familiar voice behind us.

"Hello, darlings!"

We turned. To our shock, it was Meera. I couldn't speak for a minute. I was dumfounded. Meera's last day at the conference was nothing but a recap of the previous sessions. Since many visitors had flights to catch, the conference had wrapped up early.

Meera hugged both of us from behind. She asked Rahul if he could accompany her to a friend's place that evening. As they left, I was in a state of shock. What if she had come into the room fifteen minutes later? She would have first checked the play area to find no one. Then she would have headed straight to her room. Gosh! Seeing her friend in bed with her husband would have been a disgusting sight for Meera. It would have been a disgraceful moment for me too. I wondered if I should take this as a warning or pretend that nothing would affect my relationship with Rahul.

I went back to my kids and they were excited to see me. I was surprised as I thought they would be glued to the magic show. We enjoyed the show for half an hour. Then the kids told me they wanted to play. I took them to the play area. We played for the next two hours. It was probably the best memory of the trip.

The kids were happy because their *mamma* was with them more than anything else. I helped my daughter as she struggled with her injured leg. Despite the pain, we thoroughly enjoyed the evening. This afternoon made me realise the importance of spending quality time with my children. I had always made it a point to be present around my children. But that day I realised that mere physical presence was not good enough and I had to be engaged with the little angels to make them happy. Children grow up fast and the time we spend with them is very important as we can never rewind to the past or bring back the innocent years of childhood.

But my mind kept going back and forth on how Meera must be moaning and screaming with joy. Would Rahul think of me while in bed with his wife? Would he? Yes, he would. He was thrilled a few hours ago about our possible encounter. I was thrilled too. I didn't feel jealous, nor did I miss anything.

I was happy we had not been caught naked by Meera. That would have been a disaster. This also gave me an opportunity to ponder over the most important role in my life, that of being a mother. Sex in Rahul's room would have been exciting. No doubt about that. But the valuable moments with my children were even more exciting. We wrapped up our evening and headed to the room.

Rahul and Meera planned to visit Meera's new friends from the conference. They came into my room to say goodbye. I could sense disappointment on Rahul's face. His face did not have the glint of happiness one would have after having sex. Maybe Meera and Rahul were used to having wild sex for the last two years, maybe not. Anyway, it was time to feed the kids. Madhan would arrive soon and we would go to the beach. Would he notice the glow on my face? I had had four days of fabulous sex. Would he be able to notice the change in me? Ashita's injury and Meera's early arrival had slammed the brakes on our sexual adventures. But I was happy. I had my memories to cherish.

Chapter - 13

Madhan arrived at 9 p.m. And in a manner typical of him, he asked me, "Are you all right?" I told him about our daughter. In a way I was happy about Ashita's injury. For one, it helped me from being caught red- handed. It also prevented me from basking in glory. I must be a terrible mother, I told myself. How could a mother be happy and relieved about her own daughter's injury? Even if Madhan had seen me glowing in happiness, he would certainly not have doubted me. He may have assumed that I was happy to see him or I was happy about the holiday.

However, with the burden of having an affair on my shoulders, I had to be careful. I could not take anything for granted. I was playing dual roles in my life – that of a caring wife and a mother who cared for her family and that of a mistress to a married man, taking care of her emotional needs. I needed both lives. I enjoyed playing this dual role. I hoped for it to last for a long time. I hoped Rahul would continue to love me the way he did and I hoped Madhan would continue to care for me.

I know a lot of people would call me a slut, a whore, a prostitute. We live in a world which believes the body and soul must be shared only with one person. I strongly disagree with this theory. Why can't a person fall in love with two people at the same time?

Love or arranged marriage, the enthusiasm and euphoria is short-lived. Everything lasts for two to three years or at the most five years. I challenge people who call themselves a one-woman or a one-man person. Having a physical relationship alone does not mean an extra-marital affair. There are times when we think of our past lovers, we fantasise other men and women, we may even think of someone else while making love with our partner. All these are accepted. But loving two people is not. Unfortunately, this is the kind of world we live in.

As long as these thoughts remain in my mind, it is okay. It is not okay when we act upon them. I hate the rules made by men. Yes, I think all the rules in the world are made by men. They are all biased and do not favour the instincts of the animal kingdom. Very few animals mate for life. But the mating rules are bizarre only among Homo sapiens.

A man can sleep and flirt with different women. He will not be crucified. Sometimes, it is impressive for a man to flirt. But if a woman has multiple partners or changes partners over time, she is labelled a 'slut' by the moral police. It is okay for men to satisfy their needs for physical pleasure and the thrill of being with different women. This has nothing to do with the soul or emotion. But women cannot have multiple partners for physical pleasure. They can attain that from only one person all through their lives. They don't feel the monotony or boredom of being with just one person. But society doesn't understand sex is a need for women too.

The need to have a partner is a mere reflection of an emotional need. It's a soul thing. Having sex is an offshoot of this and it comes naturally. We don't need bodies; we need emotional support.

There was no dearth of emotional support from my husband. In fact, Madhan was equal to a hundred men when it came to emotional support. Such was the love and affection of my soulmate. But I still ended up in bed with Rahul. I felt Rahul's heart with the first kiss. I knew he was there to double my emotional need. I felt a sense of fulfillment with both these men. I loved them both with all my heart and soul.

A species called the black vulture attacks the member of its group caught philandering. This way, only the most loyal partners lived. This crazy thought hit my mind suddenly.

I lay next to Madhan at the beach thinking of Rahul and Meera. It had been a while and they hadn't returned. Meera was having fun with my lover. I didn't resent it. She was lawfully his wife and was entitled to be happy with him. I thought of Rahul. Was he thinking of me, I wondered. He had a great partner in Meera. They were madly in love with each other but his soul needed more. It needed another person for complete fulfillment. All of us have a passion, be it sports, writing or music. Madhan was passionate about his business and he had this dream of becoming the number one realtor in Karnataka and, hopefully, the country someday. Meera was passionate about surgery. She wanted to become the best trauma surgeon in the country. Rahul and I were passionate about each other. We were passionate about kissing each other, passionate about making love to each other, and passionate about our souls. Alas, in this world filled with sycophants and moral police, I could not open up to anyone about my passion. I would have to live a dark life. But I was passionate about

Rahul. I believed in my passion. I didn't believe in letting go of my passion just because the world didn't believe in it.

Chapter - 14

We had a good night's sleep. We had to pack in the morning to leave for Colombo. We would spend Saturday night in Colombo, before boarding our flight to Bangalore on Sunday afternoon. Rahul and Meera did not arrive for breakfast at the usual time. I thought they may have returned to their room late at night and must still be sleeping. I called their room from the restaurant but my call went unanswered. Leaving the children with Madhan at the restaurant, I went to their room to check if everything was all right. I knocked and Meera opened the door.

Her face was bruised. She looked as though she had been crying all night. The moment she looked at me, she hugged me and burst out crying. I just held her and waited for her to calm down. The conversation that followed was the worst one I had ever had with anyone till then.

Meera began by saying that Rahul had a mistress. She said he had been having an affair with another woman for the past two years. I was stumped. I was the mistress but what's this about two years, I wondered. Meera did not know who the mistress was.

I asked her about her bruise. They had been to a house party and Rahul had gotten drunk. He had had too many drinks. When they got back to the room, they had a quarrel and Rahul had gotten a little physical.

Rahul had to send an official email. After sending the mail, he slept without closing the laptop. Meera attempted to check something on the internet. She noticed a chat window.

Meera showed me what she had seen on Rahul's laptop. The name read Deepa.

D: Hey honey, how is the Sri Lankan trip?

R: Good going, babe. What's up with you? Missing me? D: Yes, dumbo. I wish I was there with you on the beach.

How romantic that would be!

R: Same here, how I wish you could be here. It has been such boring trip. My loneliness is killing me…

D: What about your beautiful neighbour who is there with you?

R: It's great fun with her around. More details when we meet this Sunday.

D: Wow. So everything falling into place? R: I would like to believe so…

The chat went on and on. So, is this what he meant when he said he had 'office work'? Tears trickled down my cheeks slowly. How much ever I wanted to control my tears, I was unable to do so. A sense of tragedy struck my heart. A dream had just been shattered. I felt betrayed. I was no longer feeling sorry for Meera. I was feeling sorry for myself. Rahul had used me. Meera interrupted my thoughts.

"We never had a great marriage. It has been just fights and arguments. And sometimes he gets violent. I confronted him this morning and he slapped me. He just walked out and asked me to stay in the room. I did not want to tell this to anyone but seeing you now, I could not control myself. That's the reason I did not answer any calls or make it to breakfast. If he knows that I told you this, he would kill me. He was particular that you and Madhan should not know anything. He plans to tell you guys that we have an important lunch at Galle and won't be joining you in Colombo."

"Then why do you put up with him?"

"I wanted to give this marriage a chance. Earlier, it was just arguments and fights. I thought this holiday would make things better. He does not even want to have a child. It has been three months since we had sex."

This hit me hard. I couldn't believe it. I had been thinking all along that Meera was lucky to have a partner like Rahul.

My whole world came down crumbling as Meera narrated all her stories. She said Tina was not Rahul's child. She was born from her first marriage. Her husband had died due to swine flu a few years ago, when Meera was three months pregnant with Tina. Rahul's first wife had died in a road accident.

"She was from an average, middle-class family and had been married to Rahul for a year. I met Rahul at a wedding of a common friend and we started dating. Both our first marriages had ended badly. This brought us close. Slowly, Rahul got attached to my child. He was such a charmer and I loved his company."

Tell me about it, I thought to myself.

"He is not attached to Tina these days. I prefer keeping her at my parent's place most of the time and I don't want her to grow up seeing us fight daily. That is not fair on the child."

This answered my question as to why Tina did not join us on this trip.

"The first six months were wonderful and then things changed. I don't want my parents to know about this. I always thought the good days would come back. Looks like everything is beyond repair now."

"Do you know this girl Deepa?"

"No, I don't. She must be a colleague of his. I have lots to tell you, Shruthi. But you should leave now. I don't want him to see you here. I will meet you tomorrow at the airport."

I left quickly but not before forwarding some of the chat scripts to my email. In the pretext of reading them, I moved some of them to my inbox. I also deleted the forwarded mails from the sent folder. I hugged Meera and told her to stay calm.

Meera had no clue about Rahul and me.

As I walked out, I thought to myself, if Meera ever came to know that I had slept with her man, she would be heartbroken. Not because Rahul had cheated on her but because her good friend had betrayed her. While one may try to forget a stranger sleeping with your husband, it would indeed be hard to deal with a close friend's betrayal.

There was a rush of thoughts in my mind as I headed to the restaurant. Here I was, a guilty whore who stood betrayed. I was suddenly overcome with guilt that I had slept with my best friend's husband. I also realised I had been betrayed by the man I loved. I had made a terrible decision falling for a jerk like Rahul. As I walked towards my family, I looked at Madhan and realised I had betrayed him too. What would he do if my affair with Rahul was exposed? Would he hurt me or walk away from my life, taking my children away? Negative thoughts flooded my head. I sat down and tried to stay calm. Madhan asked me if everything was fine. I told him Meera and Rahul had to take care of an emergency at a friend's place in Galle and they would join us at the airport the next day.

Chapter - 15

The next two days were peaceful and quiet. I tried my best to not show any emotion that would reveal the previous day's incidents. We visited different places in Colombo. We visited the famous Buddhist temple and the Independence Park. We shopped at the popular House of Fashion mall that sold various international brands at discounted prices and later wrapped up our shopping at Odel, the upmarket mall. It was a nice family outing after which I was too tired and wanted to rest. We checked into a room at the Le Meridian hotel. The room on the sixth floor faced a beautiful beach. Madhan took the kids out. I sat on a chair in the balcony and watched the mighty ocean that was peculiarly rough that night.

Just a day ago, I thought I was as strong as the ocean. I had a sense of contentment and pride about the choices I had made in life. And here I was, just a day later, thinking about the dreaded choices I had made and the disastrous route I had taken in the name of emotion and passion. I couldn't help but think about Rahul's other side.

Just like a coin, every human being has two sides. Most of the time, we mask our real self. We do not allow our negative side to be seen. We all have a demon inside us that sleeps peacefully, waiting to be awakened. I have always believed that no soul on earth is completely dreadful. There is also no exceptionally good soul. In most of the cases, the negativity in the soul shows its ugly head when one is fulfilling his or her responsibilities and duties.

Take for instance, the politician who is so nice when he is trying to garner votes but completely ignores his people after getting elected. Or the school that puts out a big advertisement and collects a huge fee but doesn't actually give a good education to its students. Instead of sharpening a student's intellect, it ends up killing his or her creativity. Look at the sportsperson who, in the lure for money and fame, takes drugs or falls prey to match fixing and betrays his country.

Look at me, Shruthi Nair, who had such a lovely family and still went out looking for love. People like me do not have even a pang of guilt when they creep in the dark corridor, knowing too well that a demon awaits them there. The problem is that we believe that we can get away easily. The circumstances and situations favour us momentarily, making us believe that we will not cause any harm to anyone. We also think that the dark will bring with it immense joy. A sportsperson thinks there is no harm in fixing a match or taking drugs but the fact is he has denied a straightforward sports person a fair chance. The politician thinks no harm is done when he swindles public money when he could have made a world of difference to his voters.

The beast within us is always in a hurry to jump out. How we act on it determines the course our lives take. It is amazing how fear can actually contain the demon. The fear of losing face, the fear of being branded an outcast in society... This fear keeps the world where it is today.

Many of us have passion, we want to try out new things. In the process, we make mistakes. The fear in us prevents us from making mistakes. But a few idiots like me overcome that fear. We believe everything is easy and take a risk, without knowing the consequences of it. I knew all along that I was risking my life with this affair. I knew I could lose Madhan and my children forever. I knew it all along but I kept going as if nothing would happen. I enjoyed every moment I spent with Rahul. I loved him with all my heart.

For the first time, I was afraid of losing everything. I had to regroup myself. I had to ensure that I protected my relationship with Madhan. Come what may, I could not allow anything to jeopardise what I had built for a decade. I was not afraid of my affair coming out in the open. I knew it would be exposed someday. What I was afraid of, was losing my family. Losing one's family is the reason why people refrain from letting out the beast in them. Most people avoid temptation not because of loyalty alone. Of course, there is loyalty but the fear of the outcome is what prevents them from falling for temptations. It is the consequences that stop people from treading the dark path. The fear of losing their loved ones and being labelled a cheat – this is what prevents people from overstepping.

Meera decided to split from Rahul as she felt she had had enough of him. This taught me a big lesson. People like me who allow the demons inside them to dictate their lives will never know when the day of reckoning would arrive. We don't realise it could be today or tomorrow or a year later. We don't acknowledge the reality till the day actually arrives. The day we lose our love, our heart is shattered. And then we realise there isn't enough time to repair the damage done.

I slipped into bed and cried for a long time, before dozing off to sleep. I did not know when my family came back. I woke up in the morning to find them lying all around me. I was happy. For now, I was safe for I had them right next to me.

Chapter - 16

We met again at the airport and exchanged pleasantries. When Madhan enquired about the bruise on Meera's face, Rahul immediately said she had hurt herself while playing a game of gully cricket at a friend's place. He didn't know that in a few hours he would lose the most precious thing he had in his life. Rahul managed to get me alone and apologised for what happened on Friday. He still had sex on his mind. He said he would make up for it soon. He whispered into my ears, "You cannot imagine how wild that is going to be." I just smiled at him. He thought I was disappointed that we did not have sex the other day. Wow! Men! I started to wonder if his first wife had indeed died in an accident or he had done something to her. Meera and I sat next to each other throughout the flight. She told me everything about Rahul, the pain he had caused her, how he would get drunk and sexually abuse her.

Meera told me that there were days when Rahul brought his friends home. They would get drunk, while she cooked for them. Sick, I thought. I wondered how on earth a smart doctor like Meera could put up with this. She loved him, she loved her daughter. She was brought up with the right family values. She always believed she could get him back. Rahul was not worthy of her love. He didn't deserve her. And he did not deserve me. He had betrayed my trust.

Once we earn someone's trust, it gives us tremendous freedom. How many people around us are worthy of this trust? How many of us use the freedom in the manner it needs to be used? Rahul had betrayed Meera's trust and mine too. I had betrayed Madhan's and Meera's trust in me. Rahul and I were both cheats. I could not call Rahul's bluff. When you lose the trust of your loved ones, it ends up consuming everyone. It can have unimaginable consequences.

Back home, I helped Meera pack her things. She left for her parents' house while Rahul was away at work. She said she had confronted Rahul the previous night. He had promised her that he would never see Deepa again but Meera knew he was lying. I knew he was lying. He had just sent a text message to me that he couldn't wait to get wild with me.

We met at our usual hideout. Rahul was at his romantic best. How did he manage to do this? I found it difficult to be romantic with him. I enquired about Meera. He said she had gone to her parents' place for a couple of days. He invited me to his house the next day to make up for what we had missed in Sri Lanka. I refused and told him I was not prepared to take risks. We argued, fought and walked away from each other. He continued to text me but I didn't respond to him. I switched off my mobile phone. I was at crossroads. There seemed to be no smooth road in front. The journey ahead was going to be rough, very rough. For the first time in my life, I was unsure of my actions. My indecision was due to the risk of being exposed. I had to do something about it.

As Madhan was coming home late, I decided to go through the chat transcripts I had forwarded to my email from Rahul's laptop. As I read the transcript, I was shocked to find out that it had every detail of everything that had happened in Sri Lanka. It had minute details of what we had shared in bed. There was no information prior to the trip. Rahul's real face emerged. *Was he a sex maniac*, I wondered. I was in for a big shock. There was more to it than sex.

I was reminded of Murphy's law: "If you perceive that there are four possible ways in which something can go wrong and circumvent these, then a fifth way, unprepared for, will promptly develop." I had not imagined even in my wildest dreams that I would be in the middle of a storm.

The calling bell interrupted my thoughts. Madhan was back from work. I shut down the laptop. I joined Madhan. We had dinner and watched some television. I didn't talk much as Madhan was tired.

I could not believe what I had got myself into. I cried again past midnight. I couldn't sleep. I knew I was doomed. A journey that had started like a smooth and exciting ride just a few days ago had now become a nightmare. I wanted to confess everything to Madhan and cry out aloud. I wanted to hug him and let him know that I had never meant to hurt him. He was there right next to me but I could only cry helplessly in solitude.

This dread and anxiety of not knowing what was going happen to me, my family, and my future was making me paranoid. I could not discuss this with anyone. My husband would abandon me and my friend would curse me to death. God, what have you done to me? I blamed him again. Did

I not thank him for giving me all those wonderful years of sunshine and brightness? I did give him credit for the good times and I wanted him to take responsibility for my turmoil too. I was unable to figure out a way out of this mess. I prayed for a miracle. God alone could save me now.

Chapter - 17

I ignored all text messages from Rahul. He was desperate to get me in his house and get physical with me. But I had the responsibility of protecting my loved ones. They could be hurt if I did not act. I texted Rahul asking him to meet me at the Costa coffee shop near Ulsoor Lake. I knew his true colours, and I could not risk meeting him in our apartment. I did not know which way our conversation would head and how he would react. Meeting him in a public place was the safest choice. As I drove to the coffee shop, my mind went back to the contents of the chat script. I was unable to comprehend how I had missed such a big thing. Rahul was too clever and smart.

From the transcript, I gathered that Deepa was his college mate and she was going through a divorce. They planned to get married next year. In the process, they had planned to eliminate Meera. This shook me. Meera had all along been suspicious about the nature of Rahul's first wife's death. Rahul had pestered Meera about accessing the autopsy report from the hospital. A post-mortem had been conducted in her hospital and there were doubts surrounding the cause of the death – if it was an accident or murder. Meera had sneaked into the records, which showed that the doctor attending to the autopsy had raised some doubts. Rahul had silenced the hospital authorities by bribing them using his powerful contacts. Deepa's father was a district secretary in a powerful political outfit.

Rahul had wanted Meera to destroy the medical records. He had threatened to harm Meera's daughter if she did not get rid of the records. I strongly believed that Rahul had lured Meera into marriage in order to destroy the autopsy report.

While in India, Deepa and Rahul never texted or chatted with each other. They only spoke over the phone. In Sri Lanka, they did not have any other option but to chat as phone calls would have been expensive. They had planned to kill Meera in Sri Lanka on Saturday morning before we left for Colombo. Meera and Rahul had plans to go scuba diving at Hikkaduwa. But things did not go as per plan with Meera stumbling upon the chat. Now, I was not sure if Rahul had deliberately left the chat open for Meera to see, as it contained a detailed discussion of the plan to kill Meera.

But Meera hadn't read the part relating to the plan to kill her. She only knew about his romance with Deepa. She also did not know about Rahul and me. She didn't have the time and patience to go through all the chat transcripts as she was agitated. Her hopes to salvage the relationship had hit rock bottom. Rahul had hurt her because his plans had failed.

I became suspicious when I saw my name in the chat. Rahul and Deepa had spoken about my inheritance.

Rahul knew that I was my father's only daughter and I was an heir to a multi-crore empire built by my father. He had been waiting for an opportunity for two years and a momentary lapse gave him the window he needed.

Deepa knew everything that transpired between us in Sri Lanka. Rahul had mentioned about me moaning in the bath. Deepa had responded saying she couldn't wait for him to make her moan. I felt like a piece of used tissue paper. Crushed and thrown into the dustbin. I was relieved that Meera had not read any of this. I then discovered why Rahul had insisted on having sex in his room. Not for the thrill of it. He wanted to get it all on tape. Deepa and Rahul had been hatching this plan ever since the momentary lapse on Diwali. Thank goodness we did not have sex at Rahul's house or hotel room. We did make out once in his room but I hoped there was no video evidence of that. I would know soon.

I reached the Costa coffee shop a little early. I sat there waiting for Rahul. I wanted to stay positive. I believed that everything in life happened for a reason.

Why did I never have sex with Rahul in India?

Why did I refuse every time we had an opportunity in his house?

Why did I not agree to have sex in his room in Sri Lanka?

Why did my daughter injure herself on the morning I agreed to be in his room?

Why did Meera have to come early and stop us from heading to their room in the afternoon?

Why did Meera have to confide in me about Rahul's other affair and why did she allow me to see his chat transcripts?

Yes, God had his reasons. I believed in His super power.

On all the occasions, Rahul had had a plan. He had a camera in his house ready to tape me naked. If I had not spoken to Meera or had access to the chat transcripts, I would have walked straight into Rahul's trap. In fact, I had even felt bad seeing Rahul's disappointed look. I was even prepared to make up for everything once we returned from Sri Lanka.

In fact, my affair with Rahul had saved Meera. If not for my attraction for Rahul, Meera and Rahul would have gone to Sri Lanka without Madhan and me. And Rahul would have returned home without Meera. I had saved myself a huge embarrassment of being caught naked on video. The video could have been all over the internet. I couldn't imagine the shame my family would have had to endure if this had happened. My parents would have even taken an extreme step unable to bear the humiliation. Madhan too would have done something to himself and the children. I was unable to digest the fact I had nearly put my family in disgrace.

Rahul arrived. He looked somber. He immediately started talking about Meera. He accused her of having an affair with someone at work. He cooked up stories about how he found this out during the outing they had on Friday in Sri Lanka. He said when he had confronted her, Meera had walked away. I smiled at him and asked him with what moral right he could confront Meera. Wasn't the pot calling the kettle black? I asked him what he intended to do. He had already lied to me that he had had an arranged marriage with Meera. In fact, Rahul had forced Meera to say so to everyone in the apartment. He had used her only to destroy the autopsy records. She was from the trauma and accident department of the hospital and she had close access to patient files. And now that he was done with that, he wanted to move on with his sweetheart Deepa.

Meera never realised why Rahul was indifferent to her. I knew it though. Rahul acted like a loving and caring husband till Meera deleted the contentious words on the autopsy report. Once the job was done, he wanted to move on with his life. But he lingered on to dupe me. He knew about the money I would inherit. He made Deepa believe that this was their best chance to amass wealth. I wondered how long Rahul would have tried to woo me had I not fallen for him.

Rahul interrupted my thoughts. He wanted to know if I appeared low because Meera had left. I wanted to say 'yes' and make him relax. That would give me some time to think through the mess I had gotten myself into. But I couldn't get myself to lie. How far could I keep running? Things would eventually catch up with me and destroy my life and happiness. I can run but I cannot hide. I was about to confront him. I hoped the storm would pass quickly, taking away the pain, stain and guilt my affair had caused. I wanted the storm to take away all memories of his love, his kiss, and his hands that knew how to induce pleasure. I did not regret what I had done. My actions didn't cause much regret. My anguish was due to the person I had chosen. The days I spent with him ignited the passion in me, they gave me pleasure and took me back to my teenage days. Rahul had kissed my soul, whispered into my heart, and celebrated my passion. I loved and relived every moment.

I always tried to be too perfect in life. That's what my dad told me to be. He always told me that I should not settle for anything but the best. I should have let myself loose during my teenage years. My cousins and friends had a lot of fun. They seemed to be having a great life now and I seemed to have lost it all. I thought I was being smart by being a perfect little girl during my teenage years. Unfortunately, all that pent-up passion forced itself out one day, leading to my blunder. I was still trying to figure out why I did what I did but there was no good answer.

Chapter - 18

"Rahul, I want to put an end to this affair. I think it's not fair on Madhan and Meera."

Rahul looked puzzled and started to mumble.

"What, do you also want to leave me? I need you more now than ever."

"I know, Rahul. But in the interest of your marriage, it's important that we break up. I spoke to Meera and she told me about your affair. She knows there is a woman in your life and I want to ensure she only knows so much."

Rahul was confused. He was keen to know what else Meera had told me.

"She doubts your loyalty and feels there is another woman in your life. That is all she told me."

Rahul was no fool. He knew I knew much more than that "So that bitch told you everything about Deepa and me?" Rahul gave me that 'screw you too bitch' look. I could never forget those terrible eyes. The same eyes that once lit my passion were now terrifying me.

"Shruthi, I like you and I loved those steamy sessions with you. Be it making out at our hideout in the apartment or the adventurous sex we had at Bentota. I loved every bit of it." He paused to sip water. "I had an affair with you and that's it. So how does my failed marriage or me liking another girl affect what we have? Haven't you been living with two men all these days?"

This hit me hard. He was calling me a whore. I had loved Rahul with all my heart. I had not done all this for sex alone. I had given myself to Rahul not because I needed sex but because he had become my soulmate. I had to calm down. I could not show my anger to Rahul. I had to outsmart him. All he knew was I knew about Deepa. Neither Rahul nor Meera knew I had access to the chat transcripts. I had to use this to my advantage.

We left the coffee shop. Rahul wanted me to think through everything. He said he had been thinking of the missed day at the resort and wanted to make up for it. I told him I needed some time to recover and think it through.

I didn't return his calls or respond to his messages for four days. I believed the more I ignored him the closer he would get with Deepa and the faster he would disappear from my life. Meanwhile, Rahul had to deal with the process of separation from Meera. Even if he wanted to extract money from me through blackmail, Rahul would need solid evidence. What he had was not good enough.

One day, Meera called me and told me about the ugly fight at her parents' house. Rahul had come clean about our affair. Meera was sobbing all through the call. She did not shout or use foul language.

"So, did you sleep with him while I was away at the conference?" asked Meera.

I broke down.

“I am sorry, Meera. I am really sorry.” I did not want to give any justification.

“Did you sleep with him in my room in my house?”

“No, not at all. We never...”

I felt so embarrassed and dirty. I stuttered and stammered. I could not complete the sentence.

This was the toughest conversation I had had with Meera. Meera felt dejected and betrayed. She was pained. Her husband had cheated on her. With her close friend. This only made it worse for her.

I wanted to tell her about Rahul’s plan to kill her. I wanted to tell her that he had used her to destroy evidence. But I could not. I knew I would have sounded defensive and she would not have listened to me properly. It was best to leave things as they were.

Meera knew the truth, and this in a way reduced my burden. To me, this was sort of a rehearsal to what was going to happen when Madhan would find out. I couldn’t imagine how disappointed he would be. Wounds run deeper than we imagine. I reached home quickly. My in-laws were leaving for Coorg in the evening to attend a family function. I insisted that my kids accompany them. Given the volatile situation, I wanted them to be in a safe haven. I bid my in-laws and children goodbye as they left to the railway station.

Chapter - 19

My phone lit up. A message read: "Meet me at my house tomorrow at 10 a.m. Or else, at 10.05, your video will be up on the internet."

I was shocked. I thought he did not have any evidence other than some of our text messages. When did he shoot a video? I was sure it must have been in Sri Lanka. Did he place a video recorder at my hotel room? Or at our hideout? I shuddered.

I wanted Madhan badly. Madhan's busy days meant we had little time for each other. He did not even notice I was sad. I tried my best to hide my emotions. I tried to spend as much time in the kitchen with my mother-in-law or playing with my children. But I had to be rescued now. I wanted to know the direction my life was taking, if I had any future at all. I spoke to God. He didn't answer me. After all, why would anyone want to talk to me? I had betrayed my loved ones to fulfill my hunger for lust. I had tried to mask my guilt and justify my actions in the name of passion and emotion.

I had to ride out the storm. I hoped it would vanish on its own as I didn't have a solution. I waited for the pain to subside and hoped the wound would heal on its own. But the truth is, you cannot outrun fate or destiny. It had to be met head-on.

I called Rahul and told him I could not meet him in his house. I wanted to meet outside.

"You do what I ask you to do. Don't dictate terms to me. You will be here in sometime. That's it," he said.

This was the guy who never uttered a word against mine. With each passing day, Rahul's demonic side was raising its ugly head. I remembered the charming messages he used to send me from his office that would make me go weak in my knees. Like a teenage girl, I would call him when he was at work and demand that he kissed me. I knew he was at work but I would still insist. He would give me a gentle kiss over the phone. I would pretend I had not heard it and would ask him to be louder. I used to pull his legs often while he was at work. I felt immense joy like a college girl in love.

I had enjoyed all those moments. They had made me happy. I would yearn for him more and more. I would wait all day for him to return from office. We would cuddle up at our secret place and lie down holding each other, having no track of the hours that slipped by. The same lovable and charming man was now a monster in disguise.

For two years, Rahul had planned his moves cleverly. He worked from home to make sure he got my attention while Meera, Madhan and the kids were away. His interest in Zumba was just a trick to get close to me. His gentlemanly behaviour was simply to impress me. He helping me with the kids had an ulterior motive: to get hold of my wealth. Like a baffled goat, I fell prey to his tricks.

Rahul had the mind of a killer who threatened to bring everyone down with his antics. I could not allow this to happen. I had to do something about this.

That is when it hit me that he did not actually have any video evidence. This may all be a ploy to get evidence. He may be planning to seduce me and capture everything on tape.

Human beings are strange. They are ready to forgive their loved ones if there is no physical relationship involved. Having a physical relationship with another man or woman is a sin that cannot be forgiven. It calls for crucifixion. Yes, people around would be disappointed. Madhan may decide to walk out of the marriage. But I would have learnt a big life lesson.

Sure, I had confessed my sin to Meera. But I was not going to confess to anyone else. Even if Rahul did have video evidence, he was not stupid enough to let it go on the internet. At least not before he knew for sure I would not pay him any ransom in exchange for the evidence.

I recollected one of the chat transcripts from Deepa.

"No matter what, we need Shruthi till we settle down in Goa. You will never get another opportunity to get a girl of her wealth to come to bed with you. This is a one-in-a-million opportunity, so don't screw it up. Her money is the key to our success."

Sometimes in life, it is best to go with one's intuition. It gives you the strength and calmness required to tackle the turbulent times. Never ignore your instincts. I decided to go with my gut feeling.

I called up Rahul and told him I would meet him only at the coffee shop and he could upload the video on the internet if he didn't want to meet me there. His ego was hurt that I was still calling the shots. I didn't bother to wait for his response. I hung up on him. I told myself that if he believed he had a chance to milk money from me, he would not do anything stupid.

So, I met him at the coffee shop. He threatened me. He wanted me in bed one last time. He said it could be at the place of my choice. I asked him to buzz off. I was not falling for this pervert again.

I didn't trust him any longer. For a girl, trust once broken is irreparable. One could still try to make amends but the fissure will remain.

Rahul was agitated and wanted me at any cost. That is when I revealed my knowledge of the chat transcripts. I requested him to stop harassing me. I asked him straight what he wanted. Rahul was startled and started sweating profusely as I told him about his foiled plan to eliminate Meera. He went into a shell. He was dumbfounded. For a few minutes, he didn't react or say anything. I told him he was free to put up his video evidence for the whole world to see.

In turn, I threatened to go to the nearest police station and share the chat transcripts with the police. The transcripts would reveal the truth about his first wife's 'accident' and the plan to kill Meera.

Our roles had reversed. I was the boss now and I was dictating terms to him. I told him we could swim away or sink together. They say in business the bigger the investment, the better the returns. The willingness to take chances makes you rich and successful. You run the risk of losing it all but to get something big you had to think big. I was willing to take my chances though I knew that in a moment of madness, both Rahul and Deepa could harm everyone. I was not ready to lose my family. But I had to put on a brave front. I could not let Rahul have his way. I had to show him that I was prepared to drown. I was taking my chances. But as they say, fortune favours the brave.

Just then, Deepa arrived. She had been listening to our conversation sitting in her car. I noticed Rahul tap his mobile phone the minute he saw her. She gave me a big smile and introduced herself. She looked beautiful. I only wished her mind had been as beautiful as her body.

She was tall with brown eyes. Her hair was well-groomed and she wore enough accessories on her ears, neck and hands. She told me that we should cut a deal. She promised to destroy all 'evidence' and wanted me to do so too. I told her that wouldn't work as I did not trust Rahul any more. I told her to keep away from me, my family, and Meera.

Deepa looked at me and said, "Do you know about the political links my family has? I can do anything to you or your husband's business."

I didn't respond. I got up. And to her annoyance, I showed her my middle finger. And I walked away.

I did not know where I got the courage from. Maybe from some other world. I was no longer the scared hare running for cover. I was the lioness who had come out of the wild. I was going to protect my kingdom with all my might.

I knew Deepa's dad was only a district secretary. This may have threatened innocent women like Meera. But it did not scare me. In fact, my dad was one of the biggest financial supporters of several high-profile political people. Madhan's family too had connections with powerful men in politics and business. When I would not let Rahul dictate terms to me, this woman meant nothing to me. She was such a small fry.

Of course, beneath the brave façade, I was panicking. I hoped my instincts wouldn't backfire. I knew both Rahul and Deepa were capable of doing anything. They had already killed a woman; they had also planned to kill another one. It wouldn't take them long to hatch another plot. They could kidnap my kids, harm Madhan, or even release my video (if at all they had one) on the internet. I was not completely brave. I was scared too.

I thought about it hard and fast. I decided it was time to confess to Madhan. It was time to let him know the mess I was in. I had to face the consequences of my actions. I had to lift the veil off my face and show the world the real me. I had to tell Madhan that I was an unfaithful whore who was not worthy of his love.

I waited for him to come home. Tonight was going to be the toughest night of my life.

Chapter - 20

As I left for the airport, I passed by the Ulsoor Lake. I had many wonderful memories of the place. I had taken my children many times to the park there. We loved boating in the lake. Madhan and I strolled around the park on so many evenings when he would wind up work early. I passed by the Costa coffee shop where Rahul and I spent so many afternoons chatting and enjoying our love. It was also the place I ended the dreaded relationship with Rahul. I passed by our favourite Sherlock Holmes pub on Cole's road. I longed for those days with Madhan. We would drink and dance as though nobody was seeing us. There were days when we used to walk home at 10 p.m. from the pub.

I had lost it all. My mind went back to the momentary lapse. That was one moment I should have been steadfast and controlled my feelings. Instead, I had allowed my heart to dictate terms. I had been selfish to go behind my personal satisfaction. I thought I could have two parallel lives and their paths would never meet. I had wanted it all. I had it all. Now, I had lost it all.

Desire wears us out and wrecks our life. It doesn't matter how tough we are. Sometimes, desire leaves a scar that follows us everywhere. Only when you mess it up completely do you realise the need to step back and control the damage.

I sat in the plane and looked down at the earth as the aircraft soared above the clouds. How tiny the world looked, I wondered. I looked at all the buildings and tiny little human beings around. I wondered how many were going through issues of infidelity and how many had lost their loved ones forever. I saw birds afar soaring high; they could go anywhere they wanted to. I envied those birds and their lives. They had no society to worry about, no children who would need attention for several years, and no family to answer to. They just flew without a care in the world. How I wished I could soar high to a distant land that no one inhabited. I wanted to jump out of the flight, spread my wings, and fly far away from all the madness. I didn't want to die, I wanted to live. I just wanted to fly to some place far.

I reached my home in Kasturibai Nagar, at Adyar, in Chennai. The half-hour flight journey felt like a day's journey and the forty-minute ride from the airport to home felt like a four-hour ride. My mother looked at me and she was puzzled. I had just told my father that I was coming home alone. I requested them to not ask me anything or call Madhan till I reached home. I burst out crying on seeing my dad, "*Acchan*, I am sorry. Please forgive me." My mom was furious and yelled at me for walking away from my husband's house. She said that I should have gone to my in-laws' place instead.

My dad kept quiet for a moment. Looking at me, he understood the magnitude of the problem that I was in. He just hugged me and said, "You don't have to say anything, baby. I just want you to know that no matter what you did, irrespective of the magnitude of the mistake you made, you will always have me on your side. We are all human beings and human beings tend to make mistakes. Whatever you did, it doesn't matter now. You tell me everything whenever you are comfortable. Remember that this house is always there for you."

I felt great relief. My world was no longer crumbling to bits. I had found solace in my dad. As they say, no matter how old we get, girls always need their fathers. I needed his comfort badly. I needed his emotional support to negate the damage caused by Madhan walking out of my life. I needed my dad to counter the challenge that Rahul could pose in the future. I had my dad on my side and there was no way Rahul and Deepa could hurt me or cause any harm to my family.

I went straight to my room and lay down on the bed. I had to find a way to tell my dad everything. How could I tell him that I had lost my mind for a moment and that led to an affair? He certainly wouldn't want me to go into the details. So, that would certainly save me the embarrassment I went through with Meera and Madhan. But I would definitely tell him about the threat to Meera's life and the plot hatched by Rahul and Deepa to swindle money from me. I hadn't told anyone this. There were only two people whose support would help me cross the line. The first person was Madhan. With him possibly walking out of our marriage, I couldn't count on him now. I didn't have much hope after the way he reacted to my confession of my affair with Rahul. He had been so furious. I had no choice but reach out to my parents.

The other person I could depend on was my dad. His hug and comforting words were enough to assure me that I had his backing. I thought of the terrible conversation I had had last night with Madhan before I left for Chennai.

Chapter - 21

Madhan was livid when he entered the house. I did not smile at him. He looked at me with so much rage in his eyes. I knew the jackass Rahul had said something to him. Rahul's only aim was to make sure I was cornered, humiliated and left alone. He couldn't accept the fact that a woman had challenged him. He was used to getting away with a lot of things with women, including murder. I told Madhan that we needed to talk. He looked at me and asked me what was left to talk. I asked him to sit. But before I could even start, Madhan erupted. He threw a few photographs on my face. Those were obviously photographs shot by someone snooping on us. I wondered if it was Deepa.

Photographs of me with Rahul were all over the floor – pictures of us at Costa and walking around Ulsoor Lake holding hands, my mugshot taken at Rahul's house, one from our hideout, and a photo of me walking into my room at the resort in Bentota.

I looked in despair. I tried to see if there were any naked pictures of me or pictures of us kissing or making out. I did not find any. I thanked my stars. I knew Rahul did not have any evidence of us having sex. Had he possessed that, his approach would have been different. Rahul was a man on a mission. It was evident from his outburst with Meera and Madhan. He was desperately seeking revenge. I had only hurt him further by insulting Deepa. He was all out to destroy my happiness. I had to somehow tide the wave.

Madhan yelled at me. "What the fuck was going on between you two?"

"I can explain, Madhan. Please listen to me."

"You want to explain to me your adventures with another man?"

"No! Please listen to me."

"Bullshit! You want to tell your husband, the man you had been with for over nine years, that he is no longer good enough? That another body was essential to satisfy your sexual needs?"

"Oh, Madhan! Please don't talk to me like that. I want you to listen to me. I am pleading here."

"Why should I listen to you, Shruthi? We have been together for nearly ten years. You know how much opposition we had to overcome to get married. We were even willing to die for each other. And you do this after all that we had gone through?"

I broke down at this point. Yes, he was right. We had fought so hard to get married. When our parents did not approve of us being together, we had told them that we would end our lives if they did not agree to our marriage. It was only after a struggle that we ended up together. It was a triumph of true love against stiff opposition.

Madhan went on. "You have made a mockery of our struggle and love. You have not only cheated on me but have also betrayed our children. I gave you everything Shruthi. I worked so hard so that you and our children could have a luxurious life."

I sobbed and sobbed. I didn't know what to say. He was the best husband a woman could get but I squandered it all and ruined our marriage.

"Madhan, you are the reason why my heart beats. You have kept me extremely happy. I have no regrets or complaints. You have taken good care of me."

"Then why all this, Shruthi? That guy walks into my office and throws these pictures on my desk. He has the audacity to tell me that he has slept with my wife. Then he threatens me that he will ruin our lives. He says he will start circulating these photos if his needs are not met. He then walks away even before I could say anything."

This confirmed my strong intuition about Rahul. But he did not have much evidence, I reminded myself.

"Madhan, I am not justifying anything. I regret every bit of what I did but please give me a chance to explain."

"Did you sleep with him?"

Oh! This was now getting nasty, I thought to myself. "Please Madhan. Don't crucify me."

"I asked you a bloody question. Did you or did you not sleep with Rahul? Did you sleep with him in our bedroom?"

"Oh no Madhan. Not here."

"That means you slept with that bastard. Is that why you were so keen on the Sri Lanka trip? You slept with him on the same bed that we made love at the resort? This is so disgusting. I cannot digest this. Why Shruthi? You had it all and still…"

I was unable to bear it any longer. This was the situation I had dreaded the most and here it was all unfolding. I was shivering. I could not speak any longer. I wept even as Madhan continued talking.

"I made a mistake and I need redemption, Madhan. Please give me an opportunity to redeem myself."

"Redemption, my foot! What fucking redemption do you want? What fucking opportunity do you need now? Thank goodness my parents and the kids are not around. I am leaving for Coorg now and I want you gone when I return. I don't care where you go. I don't want to see you again."

"But where will I go, Madhan?"

"Well, you have your lover in the next block. Isn't that house good enough? I am sure you know the way to his house."

"God save me. Please don't do this to me, Madhan.

Please."

"Go to hell."

Those were the last words I heard from him. He walked away slamming the door on me. Madhan had never been harsh to me. Even when we argued, I would be the one yelling most of the time. Be it during our college days or after marriage, Madhan never hurt me even when we argued.

I still remembered the day I had a heated argument with his mother. I had called Madhan immediately to let him know that the joint family idea was not going to work. Those days I was always in a state of daze. With two children to feed and very little sleep, I would always be in an agitated mood. But he had been calm. Without even asking me what had happened, he promised that he would do whatever it took to make me happy.

Neither his mother nor I had been ready to give in. Caught between me and his mother, he had handled the situation with utmost maturity, responsibility and care.

Madhan later told me that both his mother and I were important to him and he could not bear to hurt or lose anyone of us. The same Madhan had now asked me to leave him forever. I knew I deserved this treatment for my adultery. Perhaps this punishment was not good enough for taking his love for granted. I only wished he had listened to what I had to say. I just sat on the sofa for the next two hours before I called my dad. It was eleven in the night and he was certainly worried.

"Chintu, is everything okay?" he asked me.

Chintu was my pet name and I loved hearing it then. I didn't speak for a few seconds and then with all the courage I broke my silence.

"*Acchan*…"

"Chintu, you don't sound fine. Please tell me what's going on."

"Please don't ask me anything. I just want to come home. Please *acchan*. I just want to come home as soon as I can."

"Okay Chintu. I will ask my travel agent to book tickets for you and the children."

"No *acchan*. It's just me. The children are with my in-laws in Coorg."

"But, why aren't you going to Coorg? Why are you coming here?"

"*Acchan*, please don't ask me anything now. I will tell you everything tomorrow. And please don't call Madhan or my in-laws till I tell you everything."

"Oh baby! What's going on?"

"Please *acchan*, just take me away from here."

In twenty minutes, I received a message from Jet Airways confirming my flight for 6.30 in the morning. In the next five minutes, I got a message from Meru Cabs about a pick-up from my house. For the first time in my life, I was alone in my house. I was surrounded by just bricks. I remembered reading somewhere: "A house is built with bricks but a home is built with hearts." My actions had taken the heart out of this house. That night was terrible. I did not sleep a wink. I questioned my actions again and again. I looked at the doorway and recollected that dreaded Diwali day when I fell into a trap. I recollected the moment of insanity that had now reduced me to a lifeless piece of flesh. I had no strength or hope left in me. I didn't know if I would survive all this. My desire and passion were now leading me to my funeral.

Chapter - 22

I woke up at 2 p.m. and freshened up. I got out of my room to talk to my dad. Mom was still angry with me but she had prepared my favourite curry. I hadn't had a bite since last afternoon. My dad said I looked weak and pale. He was not keen to listen to me talk. He asked me to have some food first. He sat next to me quietly while I had some rice and *theeyal*. Tears started to roll down my face. I choked. I could not eat. My dad comforted me and asked me to calm down. I prayed he would remain calm even after I told him about my infidelity.

I was worried because he was a man of values and he would not tolerate such behaviour from his daughter.

My dad, Vasudevan Nair, was a name to reckon with in the business and political circles of Chennai. Though he was not actively involved in politics, he gave huge donations to many political parties. He was held in high esteem due to his hard work, sincerity, and business acumen. During my teenage years, he had taught me the need to control my desires and tackle the various distractions around me. I would be a wreck if he too abandoned me.

I hoped to get back to my family. I fervently wished Madhan would have a change of heart. Till the situation improved, I wanted to take up a job and build my life again. Through all of this, I wanted my children. There was no point in living a life in which they had had no part. I had to be prepared for court battles to win custody of them. Several permutations and combinations were running through my head. Well, I had to be prepared for anything.

My dad had a meeting with someone important in the evening. After the meeting, we were to go out for dinner. My mom intervened and said she wanted everyone to stay at home. My dad then said the dinner was only for his daughter and him. I was a little upset that my dad didn't want to hear what I had to say. He knew I had walked away from my marriage and I desperately wanted to talk to him. Seeing him at home after I woke up gave me some courage. But he was not giving priority to my problem. It drove me crazy. I didn't demand attention but I was certainly disappointed that he was not even willing to listen. Given the state I was in, he was my last resort. However, beggars cannot be choosers. As the day progressed, I began to get jittery. What if dad didn't forgive me?

I was not interested in going out for dinner but I reluctantly dressed up in battered jeans and an old black tunic.

We left home at 7 p.m. and drove through the East Coast Road. I didn't know where he was taking me for dinner. And I didn't want to ask him. In the car, he enquired about my children and in-laws. He asked me if I was still taking Zumba classes. I wanted to tell him, "Dad, I am not here on a holiday or a break. I am carrying a big load of pain." But I just answered him. He stopped at the MGM Beach Resort and we headed to the seaside restaurant. Ah, the beach again, I thought to myself. It brought back the dreaded memories of the Bentota beach. My mind quickly recollected everything that happened on the trip.

That lovely night with Madhan, those intimate moments during the day with Rahul, those beautiful moments with my children, those wonderful conversations with Meera in the evenings. Alas! Those were the last beautiful moments I spent with these people. Little did I know then that I would lose them forever. The trip made me believe that life was getting better and I had everything. It was my life and I was calling the shots.

I sat at the restaurant with my dad, watching the waves. It was a full moon day and the tides were high and mighty. I wished the mighty waves would carry me into a land far away where my deeds would be forgiven and I could live happily again.

We picked up some starters from the buffet table. I got ready to talk. My dad interrupted me and asked me about Rahul. I looked at him in a state of shock.

"How do you know Rahul?"

"Just tell me about this man, Chintu," my dad said in a stern voice.

"I... well, he is our neighbour and is married to Meera. They live one block away from us."

"The family we dined with on Diwali?"

Oh yes, how could I forget?

"Yes *acchan*, he is the same person."

"Chintu, you need to tell me the truth and not hide anything from me. Do you like this person?"

"No *acchan*. I don't. He is not a nice person." "But you went around with him?"

At this point, tears started to trickle.

"Please *acchan*. I have already had this conversation with Meera and Madhan. I feel humiliated and dirty talking about it. I don't want to talk about it and definitely not with you, *acchan*. Please."

"That's okay, baby. I won't ask you about it again." My dad held my hand and I felt better.

"So, did you talk to Madhan, dad?"

"Yes. I did speak to Madhan but it's not him who told me about this." He then pulled out a packet from his suit pocket. Out came those dreaded photographs.

How did I not expect this? Rahul had sent the pictures via courier to my dad. I looked at those photos carefully to make sure they were the same ones Madhan had seen.

"Rahul called me and asked me for a ransom. He said he would ruin your life if I did not give him money. It looks like he tried the same trick with Madhan too and got an ear-full from him. His ransom call with Madhan did not work. Madhan had asked him to take a walk as he had decided to pack you out of his life. But Rahul was sure it would work with me as he thought I wouldn't want my daughter's name and image to rot on the internet. He also said he had some video evidence. He was daring enough to say, 'Of course, you are a popular name in the business world and I am sure you will want to amicably settle this and ensure the photos are hidden under the carpet forever.' What audacity!"

"What about Madhan, *acchan*? What did he say? When did you speak to him? Did he shout at you?"

"No, he did not. He tried reaching out to me last evening but I was at the club and didn't see his call. I tried to return his call but he was not reachable. I thought that all of you had left for Coorg. You then called and I knew something was wrong. He later called me at midnight and told me to take you home. I did not say anything. He wanted to explain but I just told him that I would talk later. I already knew the reason. I had seen the photographs in the afternoon itself. I did not call you immediately because I was keen on solving this myself by paying a ransom to Rahul. I initially thought he would not disturb you or Madhan if I agreed to pay, but I realised later that he had tried his luck with Madhan too."

I began to choke. The lump in my throat only got bigger and bigger each day. I began to sob.

"I am sorry, *acchan*. I have done grave injustice to you. I have sullied your name and status in society."

Dad comforted me. "Chintu, you cannot let this situation dictate terms to you. By crying, you are only allowing your emotions to take control. You need to think straight and see what you can do to overcome this crisis. Everybody goes through some crisis in life. Some people are affected by a sudden health issue; it could be cancer or a heart disease. But they cannot sit in a corner thinking that it is the end. They need to find a way to get out of the situation. Even the most powerful of people and the most intellectual ones fail in life at times.

There are people who fail in exams. They need to make sure they return prepared for the next attempt. Sportspersons prepare so hard and train with all their might. Yet, there is only one winner. The others are disappointed but they don't stop there. They go back to their training; they train harder and come back stronger.

"Everyone fumbles in life. If we were too perfect as human beings, there would be no life on this earth. Remember, there is both day and night and the world cannot survive with just one. This is life. Yes, you made a mistake but that's not the end of the world. You need to fight with every bit of what is left in you to get your family back. It may seem as though you have lost your children and Madhan today, but one day you will win your family back. You need to train your mind harder. You need to keep it calm and think about how you are going to win them back. You got to do what you have to do."

My dad's words gave me confidence. I started to believe that I could win Madhan back. My love for him was true. At no point in time did I doubt that. I was sure that he knew I loved him. That was why he was angry with me. His anger was justified because when you are truly in love with someone, you don't mess around with their feelings. I had done just that.

We were soon done with dinner. I asked my dad if we could walk along the sands of the beach. He agreed. I rested my head on his arms as we took a quiet walk. It was a beautiful night. I asked him why he was not angry with me.

"Dad, you knew about all this even before I told you. You had seen the photographs. You still stayed so calm and composed when I called you. Even when I reached home, you did not show any anger."

"Everyone makes mistakes, my girl. You should repent for your mistakes sincerely and be willing to learn from them. I realised that you had never tasted failure in life or seen disappointment. You had always got what you wanted. You had everything in life. Losing your family is the first loss you have seen. In a way, I am to blame for not letting you face failure while you were growing up. I was so keen on you succeeding always. But failure is an important tool for every human being."

He paused and then continued.

"You were the best in your class in school and a topper in college too. You got to marry the man of your choice. Then you had two lovely children. Well, that is one hell of a successful life. To me, this is just a minor jolt in your life. I am confident that you will come out of this. Failure is inevitable and unavoidable. What you need to remember is failure should never have the last word. This is just a phase. You need to hold on till then. It may take days, months or years for everything to become normal again but you need to hold on. Stand firm on your ideals and never give in or give up. I don't want you to worry about all this. I am going to make sure everything becomes fine."

"But *acchan*, you haven't answered my question. Aren't you furious?"

"No Chintu baby. I am not angry. When you are my age, you will learn to forgive easily. And when it is the most precious person in your life, the person you consider your lucky charm, your biggest asset, and the most valuable treasure, there is no question of holding a grudge."

That evening with my dad was probably the best one I had ever had with him. He gave me more than a whiff of hope. He made me feel that life was worth living. He made me realise that true love was worth fighting for. As we got into the car, I thanked the Almighty. God had certainly been kind to me. How else could I explain my dad's kindness? He could have easily disowned me to protect his social status and prestige. In all the despair and gloom, God had shown me the light at the end of the tunnel.

I told my dad that I wanted to hear my children's voice.

When we reached home, my dad called up Madhan and enquired about the children. I heard my children talk as *acchan* put them on speaker. I had heard their voices ever since they started speaking but that day their voices were more precious than ever. I talked to them for a long time. They missed me and wanted me there. I told them I had some work and I would join them soon. I had thought it would take a long time before I could hear their voices again. But Madhan had been kind enough to allow them to speak to me.

My dad then spoke to Madhan for some time. He told him he would call again in the morning. Madhan had great respect for elders and was always courteous with them. I hoped tomorrow would be a better day – the day when Madhan returned to my life. I was confident that my dad would talk him out of our separation and make our marriage work. I knew the wound would take a long time to heal but the process of healing had to start. The sooner, the better. I went to sleep with hope. I hoped for a new beginning. I wanted to let go of the past and embrace the future with my family. I knew Madhan would need time to get over everything. I was willing to wait for however long it took. Like my dad said, it could take days, weeks or even years. It would be worth the wait if I could secure my future with the love of my life.

Chapter - 23

I was lying in a pool of blood. I could hear people screaming around me. Someone was calling for an ambulance; someone was calling the police. I heard vehicles passing by.

There were too many people around me. I was not able to breathe, I was suffocating. Then I heard an ambulance's siren. Someone lifted me and moved me into the ambulance. What was happening? I was being wiped, maybe there was too much blood. It hurt. It was painful. I could not move. There was something on my face, around my nose. I think it was the oxygen mask. I heard someone shouting in the local Tamil language, "Move faster. Faster please. Fortis Malar hospital is just 2 km from here." Those were the last words I heard. There was a man inside the ambulance who kept telling me to stay awake. I was finding it difficult to keep my eyes open. The man kept talking. I saw some people move me out of the ambulance. It was all a blur. I could see people in white clothes. People were shouting all around.

"Move, move. Please give way."

"Please take her to the OR immediately." "Give way, move please."

"Madam, please stay with us. Madam, can you hear me?"

Someone was screaming into my ears. I was trying my best to keep my eyes open.

"Please call Dr Anandan and Dr Kannan."

"There is too much of blood loss, sir. She is very critical."

"Is there someone with this lady?"

"No sir. We have informed the Adyar police station."
"Let's arrest the blood flow first. Then I want you to..."

Those were the last words I heard. The next thing I knew was I was lying on a bed. I didn't know for how long or how many days I had been on the bed. I could not see because my eyelids felt very heavy. I was unable to open my eyes. I could only hear voices.

"Ms Shruthi, can you hear me? Your family is waiting outside. You have to wake up for them."

How I wished I could, kind lady, I thought. I was dying to see them all.

Suddenly, I felt someone holding my hands. There were two people on both sides of the bed. I felt a familiar stroke on one hand. Oh what a relief to have them finally, I thought. The two pillars of my life and my rock solid support. Here they were, Madhan and my dad. They didn't say anything. They did not have to. Madhan was stroking my hand and that felt so good. That was enough for me. I hoped he had forgiven me. Or had he come because I was counting my last days? I heard a nurse tell her colleague that morning, "There is too much internal damage in the head and her legs. It is just four days or at the most a week. It's difficult for her to survive beyond that. Dr Anand said if she does survive, it would be a miracle."

Madhan and *acchan* sat quietly next to me for some time. A woman interrupted us and asked them to leave. I wanted to hug Madhan, I wanted to cry and beg for his forgiveness.

"I am sorry, baby. I love you," said Madhan. His voice was all coarse. I didn't know if he was crying. Maybe he was.

"Don't cry for me, honey. I don't deserve your tears," I wanted to tell him.

I heard the doctors talk. I heard that it had been a week since I came to the hospital. I heard the doctor tell Madhan that there was a slight improvement in my health but it was not good enough. I heard the door creak and the sound of footsteps fading into the hallway. I also heard the sound of footsteps approaching me. Someone came close to me and held my hand. I felt relieved. This was something I had been waiting for. Even though my eyelids were closed, I longed for his presence. He sat next to me and said, "I love you, Shruthi."

Oh my God, thank you. This was enough. I could now rest in peace. I knew I was not going to make it. But I did not want to die not knowing if Madhan loved me or not. I hoped he would forgive me. Instead he asked for my forgiveness. He apologised for not staying with me when I wanted him the most. I wanted to tell him he was not responsible for anything and that I was solely responsible for my state and for putting my family through trauma and grief. But I could not talk.

Madhan continued.

"Shruthi, I know you are listening to me. I want you to know that I have forgiven you. I also want you to know that I am not doing this because you are in a hospital bed, which was the last place I had expected to see you. But even before your hospitalisation, I had decided that I would fly down with the kids, leave them with your parents, and spend some time with you in Pondicherry. I had booked a cab and made the resort reservations as well. Little did I know that I would see you in this condition! I knew about this only after I reached the Chennai airport. I should have stayed calm that night. I shouldn't have walked away leaving you alone. It was stupid of me to not know the danger looming over your head. I was furious that you had shared yourself with some other man. I had the right to be angry but I should have stayed, fought it out, and not walked away. I just want to let you know that most human beings on this earth don't lead a truthful life. I work day in and out to make money and how do I do that? I lie to my customers to improve my sales. I bribe government officials to get my work done. There are others who cheat during exams. Then there are the so-called professionals from the corporate world who fudge bills to get tax benefits.

"In this very hospital, doctors may be forced to lie to the families of patients. Just because bribing and lying do not bother the society, it does not make my actions right. Just because your unfortunate affair with Rahul got a few tongues wagging, it does not make you a terrible family woman. Look at our college mate Vipin. He was such a perfect person. He is now undergoing rehabilitation for alcohol and drug addiction. I can go on with more examples but you must know that every human being has some weakness or the other. You had a picture perfect life. You were a great daughter, a passionate lover, a lovely wife, a wonderful mother, and an amazing daughter-in-law. There was no fault in you. But God doesn't allow human beings to be this perfect. He takes us through trials and tribulations. He tests us. Setbacks and weaknesses such as loss in business, alcohol addiction, ego, and misunderstanding with loved ones alter your life's journey. These are all his ways of testing us. We are human after all and sometimes we lose control.

"I don't believe what the doctors say. You are a strong woman. You need to come out of this. I need you. I need you like never before. I will never get a more affectionate wife than you. Our children will never get another perfect mother. I love you and I forgive you. Come back, baby. Don't leave me."

Tears started to trickle down my eyes. Madhan gently wiped them away. He kissed my forehead and asked me to take rest. I wanted to live. This was not the time for me to leave the world, the beautiful world of Madhan, my children, and my parents. I wanted to make up for my betrayal. I started thinking of the day that led me to the critical care unit of the hospital.

Chapter - 24

Dad called Madhan and spoke to him for a long time on Saturday morning. He then told me what had transpired. Madhan was better now and wanted some time to recoup. My dad told me that it was wise to let him calm down and allow him to think it through.

"Chintu, if someone is yours, they will always be yours and they will come back. If they don't come back, they never were yours in the first place." I was confident that one day I would be back in the arms of my sweetheart.

My dad left for his weekly review meeting. I was helping my mom clean the wardrobe. My mom too had cooled off and returned to being the friend she had always been. I checked my phone for messages. Just then a video from a new number flashed on WhatsApp. I opened it. It was a video that would doom my life. It was a video of me with Rahul. He had not been threatening. He did have video evidence. I could not believe I was back to square one. We had made out once at his house and this had been captured on video.

It was a few weeks after Diwali. I was strolling around in the garden in my new blue printed jumpsuit.

I was chatting with a friend when Rahul sent me a message asking me to meet him in his house. He was talking to someone over the phone as he opened the door. When I entered his house, he kissed me and asked me to sit on the sofa. Since this was our early days, I was nervous. Once he was done with the phone call, he took me in his arms gently and kissed me all over. I was thrilled with my new life and my new partner. Nervousness turned into euphoria. Rahul then took a step back and said he wanted to charge his mobile phone. I held him by his collar and asked him if that was necessary. He laughed and walked towards the TV stand opposite the couch where we were seated. He then placed his phone on the stand and came back.

Now it made sense. He had switched on the video camera on his mobile phone to capture the moment. We made out for about five minutes. I remembered that afternoon when he gently caressed me and kissed me all over.

Though the video was not very clear, on close examination one could make out my face. I knew Rahul was rolling the last dice on the board.

This video could disrupt a possible reconciliation with Madhan. It is one thing to know that your partner slept with someone but it is entirely gruesome to actually see your partner in a compromising position with someone else. It is very difficult for the human brain to digest visual information. My actions were not just unexpected; they were also startling. Madhan and my dad had seen just casual pictures of Rahul and me. But this video was ghastly. I had been caught unaware. I had always been cautious but the one time I made out with Rahul at his place proved to be a costly mistake.

How foolish of me to have thought that I could get away with this affair! I realised that you can fool some people sometimes but you cannot fool all the people all of the time. I had made a fool of myself and put my family in an awkward position. I could tell my dad about the video. Or I could go to the police. While this would probably put an end to Rahul's bullying, it would not help me.

If my family comes to know about the video, they would be crushed. I could not let that happen. What if Rahul uploaded the video on the internet or shared it with Madhan or my dad? He would definitely do it. He was keen to bring me and my family down. This would shame my family forever. My parents and Madhan's parents had a very good reputation in society.

I did not come out of my room for the next three hours. I had to make a decision. I didn't have time to cry or worry about the consequences. Rahul was no longer willing to wait. But I didn't want to give in to his demand for money. There was no guarantee that he would stop there. I also did not know if he had a copy of the video. I had snubbed him on a few occasions and I knew he wanted to give it back to me in the same measure. He had given me time till 5 p.m. to be in his hotel room.

I reached the lobby of Savera hotel on Dr Radhakrishnan Road in Mylapore. I took the lift to the third floor as instructed. I looked around for room 313 and knocked. There he was, the man who had wrecked my life. He was wearing a light blue collarless T-shirt and three-quarter *khaki* pants.

"You are a smart girl, Shruthi. I am glad you chose to come alone. If this doesn't go as per plan, I am just a click away from letting the world know. Ah, what a shame that would be!"

"What do you want, Rahul?"

"You and, of course, a portion of your wealth. I will give you the details of my requirements later. For now, you will do."

He sat next to Deepa on the bed. She was dressed in blue jeans and a light green embroidered *kurta*. They were both sipping vodka. The vodka bottle was placed on an adjacent table.

I stood next to the window. I didn't look at them. "Shruthi, I am not going to force you. You have ten minutes to decide."

Deepa walked across and sat on the couch.

I wait for some time. I then wiped my tears. I wanted to end this today quickly. As I turned to talk, Rahul held me from behind and started kissing my neck. I tried to pull away. I was not going to give in. But he pushed me away and I fell on the table hurting myself in the process. He lifted me and held me by my neck. His strong hands hurt me.

"So, what the hell were you thinking when you showed Deepa your fucking middle finger? You thought you were being clever, bitch? Now, show me your smartness."

Deepa was watching all this from the couch with a wicked smile. Both Rahul and Deepa were high on alcohol. I wondered if the situation was going to get out of hand.

Rahul slapped me and threw me on the bed. He pounced on me and started to molest me. He squeezed my breasts hard. I started screaming. Rahul grabbed a towel and shoved it in my mouth before continuing to smother me.

"This is not new to us, baby. Why are you making it difficult? Don't you know when rape is inevitable, you should just enjoy it? Now make some noise, baby. I love to hear you moan. Are you shy because Deepa is around? Come on, she too will join us. Threesome will be awesome." Rahul chuckled and Deepa laughed.

He tried to take my clothes off. I was unable to get him off my body. I finally gained composure and gathered all my strength to hit him on his crotch with my knees. He fell off the bed. I tried to run but he was already on his toes and quickly went to the door. He would not let go of me.

I didn't think he would videotape this encounter. I had underestimated Rahul and clearly misread the situation. I guessed Deepa would be in the room but I thought this was going to be just a negotiation meeting.

Rahul was uncontrollable and yelling at the top of his voice. Deepa turned out to be a third-rated tramp.

I promised them that I would arrange for any amount of money. I pleaded with Rahul to leave me alone. As he tried to get closer to me, I lost my balance. I leaned towards the window, which had not been bolted. I had to do this. Rahul was in no mood to listen. I placed one leg outside the window. Rahul paused to see what I was doing. I regained my composure and warned him.

"Rahul, back off or I will jump out of this window." "You wench! Are you trying to fool me? You can no longer choose what happens. I set the rules."

Deepa and Rahul didn't seem to be convinced that I would jump.

"Shruthi, what do you think you are doing? Why don't you just cooperate, darling?' Deepa tried to pacify me.

"Please leave me alone and I won't say a thing to anyone about what happened here."

"Balls to you, bitch! You can go tell the whole world about this," Rahul shouted at me.

I knew they couldn't capture anything that was going on. They were desperate for my cooperation.

Deepa asked Rahul to shut up. She then turned towards me and said they would spare me any physical torture. She wanted me to calm down and come away from the window. I didn't trust her.

Deepa realised I would not budge an inch.

"That video will be of no use if I jump right now. And don't forget, my husband and dad will not spare you."

"So, are you trying to threaten us now? Let me see what the fuck you are capable of. By the way, if you think you are so daring why not just jump?" Deepa yelled at me, "The ball is in our court, you whore. You will play the game the way we want it to be played."

I had by now decided what I wanted to do next. I thumped my right fist hard on the window, nearly causing the glass to crack.

I screamed, "Remember morons, this will always remain my fucking game. I started this and I will end it. It is over when I say it is over."

Rahul realised what I was about to do and tried to catch me. I smiled at him and let go of myself. I could see both of them watch me in dismay from above, as I floated in the air. My body flipped in the air many times before my legs hit a car, causing terrible pain. And even before I could realise anything, my head hit the ground hard.

Chapter - 25

I lay still in my bed. It had been ten days since I had come to the hospital. Sometimes I heard them say, "She is improving." And then I heard, "This can be difficult and we cannot keep her on life support for too long." I was losing hope. Madhan spent a few minutes with me every day in the morning and evening. He would speak to me about our college days, our honeymoon, our children, and all the fun times we had. He would often talk about how hard we had fought with our parents to get married. We had never spent so much time in a long time. It was not often that he did all the talking with me just listening.

My dad would talk about only one thing – to get my life back. My little ones were too young to comprehend the situation. They visited me twice a week. All they would ask was, "*Mamma*, when will you wake up? Let's go home, it's boring here." I wished I could just get up and hold them in my arms and get back to my paradise.

Meera visited me twice. She had forgiven me and told me that she had now moved to Gurgaon with her child. I was glad to have all my loved ones back in my life. However, this happiness was going to be short-lived and they would soon have to cope with my absence. I had not been fair on them.

I had made a mistake and they had to pay a huge price for it. I had taken God's kindness for granted. I thought I could always have it my way.

In hindsight, I asked God why he had to test me in this manner. I talked to him. "You could have given us a loss in business or given me health issues. Or you could have delayed the birth of my children. Or even worse, I could have been childless. Why did I have to commit adultery? I had been infallible all my life. I had defied all odds to come out victorious. I had seen many laurels in life. I had been a loving daughter, a meritorious student, and a happy and caring wife and mother. I had also been a hot mistress in bed. I could cook the must sumptuous food and I also sometimes helped my husband in his business. Is it my fault that I strived to be the best in all that I did? Did I challenge your position as God and is that why you had to bring me down? I am not going to ask you to bring me back to life. I will not beg you to keep me alive. I want to meet you and ask you all these questions. I am not denying my mistake. But you never gave me an opportunity to fail all my life. And then I made one blunder and now I cannot come out of it alive."

I felt some discomfort in my upper stomach. I started to sweat. I was not able to breathe, despite the oxygen mask. I heard noises around.

"She is falling. Can someone call for Dr Anand?" "Oh no. Her pulse is weak. I need more attendants." "Vanaja, start CPR. Charge to 100."

The noises then seemed to fade away slowly as though they were from a place far away. I felt I was entering a passage. It was pretty dark and I was afraid to step in. I got into it nevertheless. I kept walking. Strangely with each step forward, I felt elated. Is this what they called the way to the other world? Would I meet my creator? Then I felt a huge thud on my chest as if I had had some kind of an electric shock.

Chapter - 26

Two years later…

Madhan and children are playing in the lush gardens of GRT Beach Resort in Mahabalipuram. The view of the sea from the resort is gorgeous. The shore looks alluring.

The sea is intriguing and exciting. It always reinforces in me a sense of belonging. The waves bring with them a strange kind of peace and calm. The sea has been a silent spectator to many major incidents in my life. Through melancholy and bliss, this magnificent body of water has given me the kind of courage that no human being could ever give. It has embraced me during the most challenging moments in my life. All my worries dissolve in the foamy waters of the unending ocean.

Here I am, admiring the stretch of splendour again. My kids run towards me, jump on me, and throw sand all over me. They laugh and squeal for the umpteenth time in the last two days. Their excitement is contagious and I laugh along with them. Madhan is just a few feet away, clicking pictures. The three of them are relieved to see me stand and function by myself after days of immobility and dependence.

I was in coma for forty-five days. I spent another three months in several hospitals. My family consulted doctors in three multi-specialty hospitals in Chennai and Mumbai before

I started to recover. My legs took a while to heal completely. I started walking about two months ago.

It is Diwali time. We decide to spend this Diwali with my parents in Chennai. This is the first Diwali we are spending together after the disastrous one in Bangalore. I cannot erase the memory of that dreaded Diwali day that nearly destroyed everything I had. I had kissed death before returning to this world. In the process, I had given my family and loved ones a harrowing time, something they did not deserve at all. In all this, I thank God for his kindness.

While I question God on why he made me go through the entire ordeal, I also thank him profusely for protecting me and my family. I thank God for giving me the sense to not make out with Rahul in public.

Something had prevented me from agreeing to have sex with Rahul in his room at the resort in Sri Lanka. Ashita hurting her leg and Meera wrapping up her conference early were signs from the power above. The chat transcripts saved Meera's life. There was God's work in everything. Divine intervention had protected me all the way through the storm.

But why did I bring all this upon myself? Why did I let go off my values? I do not have answers to these questions. Some things are beyond human comprehension. We just need to let go and trust that everything will be okay.

At the beach resort, I join my dad for a walk along the shore. I ask him the same questions.

"Why does God do all this? Who decides our fate? Where does he go during times of turbulence, when we fail? I don't see him at all."

My dad tells me that it is human to make mistakes and God lets us make mistakes.

"What's important is we realise our mistakes and get back to the path of good."

He then tells me something he had read.

"A person had a dream once. It was during his happier days. There were two pairs of legs on the shore. One was his and the other was God's. However, during the testing times he could see only one pair of legs. He cried and asked God how he could leave him alone and go away. God quietly answered, "I was playing with you during your happy times, walking by you side by side. During hardships, the pair of legs you saw were that of mine. I was carrying you."

I smiled and thanked God for carrying me for the last two years.

Dad then enquires about Meera. I tell him that we met recently in Bangalore.

"She is now dating a doctor who works with her. He seems to be a nice person. She is living happily in Gurgaon."

I do not know the whereabouts of Rahul or Deepa. They have not disturbed me since that dreadful day. They have not made any ransom calls to Madhan or my dad. The Bangalore police enquired us about them after a complaint from their parents and friends. Meera too has not heard from him. She isn't bothered about him.

I cannot help but think of Rahul now and then. For two years, he had made his moves well. Luck favoured him and I fell for him. Despite his cunning nature, he had a nice side to him too. In his company, I had always been cheerful. I do not love him any longer but I had once given myself to him. I cannot erase his memory completely. Had he not been greedy, he would have made a good father and a good husband to Meera. I still worry about the video. It still gives me nightmares.

I ask my dad if he knows anything about Rahul and Deepa. Dad looks at me and holds me closely in his arms.

"Chintu, I don't want to answer this but I want you to know that no one will ever hurt you as long as I am around."

I become suspicious with this response and ask him if he has done something to them.

He doesn't say anything. He just smiles and this irritates me.

"Acchan, please tell me. Where are they? Did you settle a ransom or hurt them or even kill them? I know you wouldn't have killed them."

He smiles again. "I am not telling you anything, Chintu." I know for certain that my dad has something to do with their disappearance. I don't know what he has done to them.

No matter how much I ask, acchan just smiles. Well, it is a reassuring smile.

Thank you for reading this book.

I hope you have enjoyed this story.

You can contact the author

Blog

https://eiramoni.wordpress.com/

https://jagdishjoghee.wordpress.com/

Twitter handle

https://twitter.com/JagdishJoghee

Facebook Page

https://www.facebook.com/jagdishj

Goodreads page

https://www.goodreads.com/author/show/14421090.Jagdish_Joghee

Google+ Id

https://plus.google.com/+JagdishJoghee

Instagram

https://www.instagram.com/jagdishjoghee/